LAO TZU, meaning "Old Master," was a Chinese philosopher, who was believed to be an older contemporary of Confucius, and the founder of Taoism, one of the three great religious and philosophical traditions of China. A record keeper in the court of Zhou in the 6th century B.C., Lao Tzu has been credited as the author of *Tao Te Ching*, though the identity of this seminal Taoist treatise's author(s) or compiler(s) is still widely debated. In the tradition of most ancient Chinese philosophers, Lao Tzu often takes recourse to paradox, analogy, repetition, symmetry, rhyme, rhythm, and appropriation of ancient sayings, to explain his ideas.

JAMES LEGGE (1815-1897) was a Scottish sinologist, scholar and missionary, who translated Classical Chinese texts into English. He served as a representative of the London Missionary Society in Malacca and Hong Kong (1840-1873) and was the first Professor of Chinese at Oxford University (1876-1897). In association with Max Müller, he prepared the monumental *Sacred Books of the East* series, published in 50 volumes between 1879 and 1891.

TAO TE CHING

AND ITS CHARACTERISTICS

Lao Tzu

Translation and commentary by
James Legge

Om Books International

Reprinted in 2025

Om Books International

Corporate & Editorial Office
A-12, Sector 64, Noida 201 301
Uttar Pradesh, India
Phone: +91 120 477 4100
Email: editorial@ombooks.com
Website: www.ombooksinternational.com

Sales Office
107, Ansari Road, Darya Ganj,
New Delhi 110 002, India
Phone: +91 11 4000 9000
Email: sales@ombooks.com
Website: www.ombooks.com

ISBN: 978-93-5376-548-4

Printed in India

10 9 8 7 6 5 4 3

Contents

PART I

PART II

PART I

1

1\. 1. The Tâo that can be trodden is not the enduring and unchanging Tâo. The name that can be named is not the enduring and unchanging name.

2\. (Conceived of as) having no name, it is the Originator of heaven and earth; (conceived of as) having a name, it is the Mother of all things.

3\. Always without desire we must be found, If its deep mystery we would sound; But if desire always within us be, Its outer fringe is all that we shall see.

4\. Under these two aspects, it is really the same; but as development takes place, it receives the different names. Together we call them the Mystery. Where the Mystery is the deepest is the gate of all that is subtle and wonderful.

體道, 'Embodying the Tâo.' The author sets forth, as well as the difficulty of his subject would allow him, the nature of the Tâo in itself, and its manifestation. To understand the Tâo one must be partaker of its nature.

Par. 3 suggests the words of the apostle John, 'He that loveth not knoweth not God; for God is love.' Both the Tâo, Lâo-dze's ideal in the absolute, and its Teh, or operation, are comprehended in this chapter, the latter being the Tâo with the name, the Mother of all things.

2

2. 1. All in the world know the beauty of the beautiful, and in doing this they have (the idea of) what ugliness is; they all know the skill of the skilful, and in doing this they have (the idea of) what the want of skill is.

2. So it is that existence and non-existence give birth the one to (the idea of) the other; that difficulty and ease produce the one (the idea of) the other; that length and shortness fashion out the one the figure of the other; that (the ideas of) height and lowness arise from the contrast of the one with the other; that the musical notes and tones become harmonious through the relation of one with another; and that being before and behind give the idea of one following another.

3. Therefore the sage manages affairs without doing anything, and conveys his instructions without the use of speech.

4. All things spring up, and there is not one which declines to show itself; they grow, and there is no claim made for their ownership; they go through their processes, and there is no expectation (of a reward for the results). The work is accomplished, and there is no resting in it (as an achievement).

The work is done, but how no one can see; 'Tis this that makes the power not cease to be.

隨, 'The Nourishment of the Person.' But many of Ho-shang Kung's titles are more appropriate than this.

The chapter starts with instances of the antinomies, which suggest to the mind each of them the existence of its corresponding opposite; and the author finds in them an analogy to the 'contraries' which characterise the operation of the Tâo, as stated in Ch. 40. He then proceeds to describe the action of the sage in par. 3 as in accordance with this law of contraries; and, in par. 4, that of heaven and earth, or what we may call nature, in the processes of the vegetable world.

Par. 2 should be rhymed, but I could not succeed to my satisfaction in the endeavour to rhyme it. Everyone who can read Chinese will see that the first four members rhyme. The last two rhyme also, the concluding 隨 being pronounced so;–see the Khang-hsî dictionary.

3

3. 1. Not to value and employ men of superior ability is the way to keep the people from rivalry among themselves; not to prize articles which are difficult to procure is the way to keep them from becoming thieves; not to show them what is likely to excite their desires is the way to keep their minds from disorder.

2. Therefore the sage, in the exercise of his government, empties their minds, fills their bellies, weakens their wills, and strengthens their bones.

3. He constantly (tries to) keep them without knowledge and without desire, and where there are those who have knowledge, to keep them from presuming to act (on it). When there is this abstinence from action, good order is universal.

安民, 'Keeping the People at Rest.' The object of the chapter is to show that government according to the Tâo is unfavourable to the spread of knowledge among the people, and would keep them rather in the state of primitive simplicity and ignorance, thereby securing their restfulness and universal good order. Such is the uniform teaching of Lâo-dze and his great follower Kwang-dze, and of all Tâoist writers.

4

4. 1. The Tâo is (like) the emptiness of a vessel; and in our employment of it we must be on our guard against all fullness. How deep and unfathomable it is, as if it were the Honoured Ancestor of all things!

2. We should blunt our sharp points, and unravel the complications of things; we should attemper our brightness, and bring ourselves into agreement with the obscurity of others. How pure and still the Tâo is, as if it would ever so continue!

3. I do not know whose son it is. It might appear to have been before God.

無源, 'The Fountainless.' There is nothing before the Tâo; it might seem to have been before God. And yet there is no demonstration by it of its presence and operation. It is like the emptiness of a vessel. The second character = 沖 = 盅 ;–see Khang-hsî on the latter. The practical lesson is, that in following the Tâo we must try to be like it.

5

5. 1. Heaven and earth do not act from (the impulse of) any wish to be benevolent; they deal with all things as the dogs of grass are dealt with. The sages do not act from (any wish to be) benevolent; they deal with the people as the dogs of grass are dealt with.

2. May not the space between heaven and earth be compared to a bellows?

'Tis emptied, yet it loses not its power; 'Tis moved again, and sends forth air the more. Much speech to swift exhaustion lead we see; Your inner being guard, and keep it free.

虛用, 'The Use of Emptiness.' Quiet and unceasing is the operation of the Tâo, and effective is the rule of the sage in accordance with it.

The grass-dogs in par. 1 were made of straw tied up in the shape of dogs, and used in praying for rain; and afterwards, when the sacrifice was over, were thrown aside and left uncared for. Heaven and earth and the sages dealt so with all things and with the people; but the illustration does not seem a happy one. Both Kwang-dze and Hwâi-nan mention the grass-dogs. See especially the former, XIV, 25 a, b. In that Book there is fully developed the meaning of this chapter. The Chinese bellows is different to look at from ours, but the principle is the same in the construction of both. The paragraph concludes in a way that lends some countenance to the later Tâoism's dealing with the breath.

6

6. The valley spirit dies not, aye the same; The female mystery thus do we name. Its gate, from which at first they issued forth, Is called the root from which grew heaven and earth. Long and unbroken does its power remain, Used gently, and without the touch of pain.

成象, 'The Completion of Material Forms.' This title rightly expresses the import of this enigmatical chapter; but there is a foundation laid in it for the development of the later Tâoism, which occupies itself with the prolongation of life by the management of the breath (氣) or vital force.

'The valley' is used metaphorically as a symbol of 'emptiness' or 'vacancy;' and 'the spirit of the valley' is the something invisible, yet almost personal, belonging to the Tâo, which constitutes the Teh (德) in the name of our King. 'The spirit of the valley' has come to be a name for the activity of the Tâo in all the realm of its operation. 'The female mystery' is the Tâo with a name of Ch. 1, which is 'the Mother of all things.' All living beings have a father and mother. The processes of generation and production can hardly be imaged by us but by a recognition of this fact; and so Lâo-dze thought of the existing realm of nature–of life–as coming through an evolution (not a creation) from the primal air or breath, dividing into two, and thence appearing in the forms of things, material and immaterial. The chapter is found in Lieh-dze (I, 1 b) quoted by him from a book of Hwang-Tî; and here Lâo-dze has appropriated it, and made it his own.

7

7. 1. Heaven is long-enduring and earth continues long. The reason why heaven and earth are able to endure and continue thus long is because they do not live of, or for, themselves. This is how they are able to continue and endure.

2. Therefore the sage puts his own person last, and yet it is found in the foremost place; he treats his person as if it were foreign to him, and yet that person is preserved. Is it not because he has no personal and private ends, that therefore such ends are realised?

韜光, 'Sheathing the Light.' The chapter teaches that one's best good is realised by not thinking of it, or seeking for it. Heaven and earth afford a pattern to the sage, and the sage affords a pattern to all men.

8

8. 1. The highest excellence is like (that of) water. The excellence of water appears in its benefiting all things, and in its occupying, without striving (to the contrary), the low place which all men dislike. Hence (its way) is near to (that of) the Tâo.

2. The excellence of a residence is in (the suitability of) the place; that of the mind is in abysmal stillness; that of associations is in their being with the virtuous; that of government is in its securing good order; that of (the conduct of) affairs is in its ability; and that of (the initiation of) any movement is in its timeliness.

3. And when (one with the highest excellence) does not wrangle (about his low position), no one finds fault with him.

易性, 'The Placid and Contented Nature.' Water, as an illustration of the way of the Tâo, is repeatedly employed by Lâo-dze.

The various forms of what is excellent in par. 2 are brought forward to set forth the more, by contrast, the excellence of the humility indicated in the acceptance of the lower place without striving to the contrary.

9

9. 1. It is better to leave a vessel unfilled, than to attempt to carry it when it is full. If you keep feeling a point that has been sharpened, the point cannot long preserve its sharpness.

2. When gold and jade fill the hall, their possessor cannot keep them safe. When wealth and honours lead to arrogancy, this brings its evil on itself. When the work is done, and one's name is becoming distinguished, to withdraw into obscurity is the way of Heaven.

運夷; but I cannot give a satisfactory rendering of this title. The teaching of the chapter is, that fullness and complacency in success are contrary to the Tâo.

The first clauses of the two sentences in par. 1, 持而 are instances of the 'inverted' style not uncommon in the oldest composition. The way of Heaven' = 'the Heavenly Tâo' exemplified by man.

10

10. 1. When the intelligent and animal souls are held together in one embrace, they can be kept from separating. When one gives undivided attention to the (vital) breath, and brings it to the utmost degree of pliancy, he can become as a (tender) babe. When he has cleansed away the most mysterious sights (of his imagination), he can become without a flaw.

2. In loving the people and ruling the state, cannot he proceed without any (purpose of) action? In the opening and shutting of his gates of heaven, cannot he do so as a female bird? While his intelligence reaches in every direction, cannot he (appear to) be without knowledge?

3. (The Tâo) produces (all things) and nourishes them; it produces them and does not claim them as its own; it does all, and yet does not boast of it; it presides over all, and yet does not control them. This is what is called 'The mysterious Quality' (of the Tâo).

能爲, 'Possibilities.' This chapter is one of the most difficult to understand and translate in the whole work. Even Kû Hsî was not able to explain the first member satisfactorily. The text of that member seems well supported; but I am persuaded the first clause of it is somehow corrupt.

The whole seems to tell what can be accomplished by one who is possessed of the Tâo. In par. 3 he appears free from all self-consciousness in what he does, and of all self-satisfaction in the results of his doing. The other two paragraphs seem to speak of what he can do under the guidance of the Tâo for himself and for others. He can by his management of his vital breath bring his body to the state of Tâoistic perfection, and keep his intelligent and animal souls from being separated, and he can rule men without purpose and effort. 'The gates of heaven' in par. 2 is a Tâoistic phrase for the nostrils as the organ of the breath;–see the commentary of Ho-shang Kung.

11

11. The thirty spokes unite in the one nave; but it is on the empty space (for the axle), that the use of the wheel depends. Clay is fashioned into vessels; but it is on their empty hollowness, that their use depends. The door and windows are cut out (from the walls) to form an apartment; but it is on the empty space (within), that its use depends. Therefore, what has a (positive) existence serves for profitable adaptation, and what has not that for (actual) usefulness.

無用, 'The Use of what has no Substantive Existence.' The three illustrations serve to set forth the freedom of the Tâo from all preoccupation and purpose, and the use of what seems useless.

12

12. 1. Colour's five hues from th' eyes their sight will take; Music's five notes the ears as deaf can make; The flavours five deprive the mouth of taste; The chariot course, and the wild hunting waste make mad the mind; and objects rare and strange, Sought for, men's conduct will to evil change.

2. Therefore the sage seeks to satisfy (the craving of) the belly, and not the (insatiable longing of the) eyes. He puts from him the latter, and prefers to seek the former.

檢欲, 'The Repression of the Desires.' Government in accordance with the Tâo seeks to withdraw men from the attractions of what is external and pleasant to the senses and imagination, and to maintain the primitive simplicity of men's ways and manners. Compare Ch. 2. The five colours are Black, Red, Green or Blue, White, and Yellow; the five notes are those of the imperfect Chinese musical scale, our G, A, B, D, E; the five tastes are Salt, Bitter, Sour, Acrid, and Sweet.

I am not sure that Wang Pî has caught exactly the author's idea in the contrast between satisfying the belly and satisfying the eyes; but what he says is ingenious, 'In satisfying the belly one nourishes himself; in gratifying the eyes he makes a slave of himself.'

13

13. 1. Favour and disgrace would seem equally to be feared; honour and great calamity, to be regarded as personal conditions (of the same kind).

2. What is meant by speaking thus of favour and disgrace? Disgrace is being in a low position (after the enjoyment of favour). The getting that (favour) leads to the apprehension (of losing it), and the losing it leads to the fear of (still greater calamity):–this is what is meant by saying that favour and disgrace would seem equally to be feared.

And what is meant by saying that honour and great calamity are to be (similarly) regarded as personal conditions? What makes me liable to great calamity is my having the body (which I call myself); if I had not the body, what great calamity could come to me?

3. Therefore he who would administer the kingdom, honouring it as he honours his own person, may be employed to govern it, and he who would administer it with the love which he bears to his own person may be entrusted with it.

厭恥, 'Loathing Shame.' The chapter is difficult to construe, and some disciples of Kû Hsî had to ask him to explain it as in the case of Ch. 10. His remarks on it are not to my mind satisfactory. Its object seems to be to show that the cultivation of the person according to the Tâo, is the best qualification for the highest offices, even for the government of the world. Par. 3 is found in Kwang-dze (XI, 18 b) in a connexion which suggests this view of the chapter. It may be observed, however, that in him the position of the verbal characters in the two clauses of the paragraph is the reverse of that in the text of Ho-shang Kung, so that we can hardly accept the distinction of meaning of the two characters given in his commentary, but must take them as synonyms. Professor Gabelentz gives the following version of Kwang-dze: 'Darum, gebraucht er seine Person achtsam in der Verwaltung des Reiches, so mag man ihm die Reichsgewalt anvertrauen; ...liebend (schonend)...übertragen.'

14

14. 1. We look at it, and we do not see it, and we name it 'the Equable.' We listen to it, and we do not hear it, and we name it 'the Inaudible.' We try to grasp it, and do not get hold of it, and we name it 'the Subtle.' With these three qualities, it cannot be made the subject of description; and hence we blend them together and obtain The One.

2. Its upper part is not bright, and its lower part is not obscure. Ceaseless in its action, it yet cannot be named, and then it again returns and becomes nothing. This is called the Form of the Formless, and the Semblance of the Invisible; this is called the Fleeting and Indeterminable.

3. We meet it and do not see its Front; we follow it, and do not see its Back. When we can lay hold of the Tâo of old to direct the things of the present day, and are able to know it as it was of old in the beginning, this is called (unwinding) the clue of Tâo.

贊玄, 'The Manifestation of the Mystery.' The subject of par. 1 is the Tâo, but the Tâo in its operation, and not the primal conception of it, as entirely distinct from things, which rises before the mind in the second paragraph. The Chinese characters which I have translated 'the Equable,' 'the Inaudible,' and 'the Subtle,' are now pronounced Î, Hî, and Wei, and in 1823 Rémusat fancied that they were intended to give the Hebrew tetragrammaton יהוה, which he thought had come to Lâo-dze somehow from the West, or been found by him there. It was a mere fancy or dream; and still more so is the recent attempt to revive the notion by Victor von Strauss in 1870, and Dr. Edkins in 1884. The idea of the latter is specially strange, maintaining, as he does, that we should read the characters according to their old sounds. Lâo-dze has not in the chapter a personal Being before his mind, but the procedure of his mysterious Tâo, the course according to which the visible phenomena take place, incognisable by human sense and capable of only approximate description by terms appropriate to what is within the domain of sense.

15

15. 1. The skilful masters (of the Tâo) in old times, with a subtle and exquisite penetration, comprehended its mysteries, and were deep (also) so as to elude men's knowledge. As they were thus beyond men's knowledge, I will make an effort to describe of what sort they appeared to be.

2. Shrinking looked they like those who wade through a stream in winter; irresolute like those who are afraid of all around them; grave like a guest (in awe of his host); evanescent like ice that is melting away; unpretentious like wood that has not been fashioned into anything; vacant like a valley, and dull like muddy water.

3. Who can (make) the muddy water (clear)? Let it be still, and it will gradually become clear. Who can secure the condition of rest? Let movement go on, and the condition of rest will gradually arise.

4. They who preserve this method of the Tâo do not wish to be full (of themselves). It is through their not being full of themselves that they can afford to seem worn and not appear new and complete.

顯德, 'The Exhibition of the Quality,' that is, of the Tâo, which has been set forth in the preceding chapter. Its practical outcome is here described in the masters of it of old, who in their own weakness were yet strong in it, and in their humility were mighty to be co-workers with it for the good of the world.

The variety of the readings in par. 4 is considerable, but not so as to affect the meaning. This paragraph is found in Hwâi-nan (XII, 23 a) with an unimportant variation. From the illustration to which it is subjoined he understood the fullness, evidently as in Ch. 9, as being that of a vessel filled to overflowing. Both here and there such fullness is used metaphorically of a man overfull of himself; and then Lâo-dze slides into another metaphor, that of a worn-out garment. The text of par. 3 has been variously tampered with. I omit the 久 of the current copies, after the example of the editors of the great recension of the Yung-lo period (A.D. 1403-1424) of the Ming dynasty.

16

16. 1. The (state of) vacancy should be brought to the utmost degree, and that of stillness guarded with unwearying vigour. All things alike go through their processes of activity, and (then) we see them return (to their original state). When things (in the vegetable world) have displayed their luxuriant growth, we see each of them return to its root. This returning to their root is what we call the state of stillness; and that stillness maybe called a reporting that they have fulfilled their appointed end.

2. The report of that fulfilment is the regular, unchanging rule. To know that unchanging rule is to be intelligent; not to know it leads to wild movements and evil issues. The knowledge of that unchanging rule produces a (grand) capacity and forbearance, and that capacity and forbearance lead to a community (of feeling with all things). From this community of feeling comes a kingliness of character; and he who is king-like goes on to be heaven-like. In that likeness to heaven he possesses the Tâo. Possessed of the Tâo, he endures long; and to the end of his bodily life, is exempt from all danger of decay.

歸根, 'Returning to the Root.' The chapter exhibits the operation of the Tâo in nature, in man, and in government; an operation silent, but all-powerful; unaccompanied with any demonstration of its presence, but great in its results.

An officer receives a charge or commission from his superior (受命); when he reports the execution of it he is said 復命. So all animate things, including men, receive their charge from the Tâo as to their life, and when they have fulfilled it they are represented as reporting that fulfilment; and the fulfilment and report are described as their unchanging rule, so that they are the Tâo's impassive instruments, having no will or purpose of their own,–according to Lâo-dze's formula of 'doing nothing and yet doing all things (無爲而無不爲).'

The getting to possess the Tâo, or to be an embodiment of it, follows the becoming Heaven or Heaven-like; and this is in accordance with the saying in Ch. 4 that 'the Tâo might seem to have been before God.' But, in Kwang-dze especially, we often find the full possessor and displayer of the Tâo spoken of as 'Heaven.' The last sentence, that he who has come to the full possession of the Tâo is exempt from all danger of decay, is generally illustrated by a reference to the utterances in Ch. 50; as if Lâo-dze did indeed see in the Tâo a preservative against death.

17

17. 1. In the highest antiquity, (the people) did not know that there were (their rulers). In the next age they loved them and praised them. In the next they feared them; in the next they despised them. Thus it was that when faith (in the Tâo) was deficient (in the rulers) a want of faith in them ensued (in the people).

2. How irresolute did those (earliest rulers) appear, showing (by their reticence) the importance which they set upon their words! Their work was done and their undertakings were successful, while the people all said, 'We are as we are, of ourselves!'

淳風, 'The Unadulterated Influence.' The influence is that of the Tâo, as seen in the earliest and paradisiacal times. The two chapters that follow are closely connected with this, showing how the silent, passionless influence of the Tâo was gradually and injuriously superseded by 'the wisdom of the world,' in the conduct of government.

In the first sentence there is a small various reading of 不 for 下, but it does not affect the meaning of the passage. The first clause of par. 2 gives some difficulty; 其貴言 'they made their words valuable or precious,' i.e. 'they seldom spake;' cp. 1 Sam. iii. 1.

18

18. 1. When the Great Tâo (Way or Method) ceased to be observed, benevolence and righteousness came into vogue. (Then) appeared wisdom and shrewdness, and there ensued great hypocrisy.

2. When harmony no longer prevailed throughout the six kinships, filial sons found their manifestation; when the states and clans fell into disorder, loyal ministers appeared.

俗薄, 'The Decay of Manners.' A sequel to the preceding chapter, and showing also how the general decay of manners afforded opportunity for the display of certain virtues by individuals. Observe 'the Great Tâo,' occurring here for the first time as the designation of 'the Tâo.'

19

19. 1. If we could renounce our sageness and discard our wisdom, it would be better for the people a hundredfold. If we could renounce our benevolence and discard our righteousness, the people would again become filial and kindly. If we could renounce our artful contrivances and discard our (scheming for) gain, there would be no thieves nor robbers.

2. Those three methods (of government) Thought olden ways in elegance did fail And made these names their want of worth to veil; But simple views, and courses plain and true Would selfish ends and many lusts eschew.

還淳, 'Returning to the Unadulterated Influence.' The chapter desires a return to the simplicity of the Tâo, and shows how superior the result would be to that of the more developed systems of morals and government which had superseded it. It is closely connected with the two chapters that precede. Lâo-dze's call for the renunciation of the methods of the sages and rulers in lieu of his fancied paradisiacal state is repeated ad nauseam by Kwang-dze.

20

20. 1. When we renounce learning we have no troubles. The (ready) 'yes,' and (flattering) 'yea;'– Small is the difference they display. But mark their issues, good and ill;– What space the gulf between shall fill? What all men fear is indeed to be feared; but how wide and without end is the range of questions (asking to be discussed)!

2. The multitude of men look satisfied and pleased; as if enjoying a full banquet, as if mounted on a tower in spring. I alone seem listless and still, my desires having as yet given no indication of their presence. I am like an infant which has not yet smiled. I look dejected and forlorn, as if I had no home to go to. The multitude of men all have enough and to spare. I alone seem to have lost everything. My mind is that of a stupid man; I am in a state of chaos.

Ordinary men look bright and intelligent, while I alone seem to be benighted. They look full of discrimination, while I alone am dull and confused. I seem to be carried about as on the sea, drifting as if I had nowhere to rest. All men have their spheres of action, while I alone seem dull and incapable, like a rude borderer. (Thus) I alone am different from other men, but I value the nursing-mother (the Tâo).

異俗, 'Being Different from Ordinary Men.' The chapter sets forth the difference to external appearance which the pursuit and observance of the Tâo produces between its votaries and others; and Lâo-dze speaks in it as himself an example of the former. In the last three chapters he has 'been advocating the cause of the Tâo against the learning and philosophy of the other school of thinkers in the country. Here he appears as having renounced learning, and found an end to the troubles and anxieties of his own mind; but at the expense of being misconceived and misrepresented by others. Hence the chapter has an autobiographical character.

Having stated the fact following the renunciation of learning, he proceeds to dwell upon the troubles of learning in the rest of par. 1. Until the votary of learning knows everything, he has no rest. But the instances which he adduces of this are not striking nor easily understood. I cannot throw any light on the four lines about the 'yes' and the 'Yea.'

Confucius (Ana. XVI, viii) specifies three things of which the superior man stands in awe; and these and others of a similar nature may have been the things which Lâo-dze had in his mind. The nursing-mother at the end is, no doubt, the Tâo in operation, 'with a name,' as in Ch. 1 the mysterious virtue' of chapters 51 and 52.

21

21. The grandest forms of active force From Tâo come, their only source. Who can of Tâo the nature tell? Our sight it flies, our touch as well. Eluding sight, eluding touch, The forms of things all in it crouch; Eluding touch, eluding sight, There are their semblances, all right. Profound it is, dark and obscure; Things' essences all there endure. Those essences the truth enfold Of what, when seen, shall then be told. Now it is so; 'twas so of old. Its name–what passes not away; So, in their beautiful array, Things form and never know decay.

How know I that it is so with all the beauties of existing things? By this (nature of the Tâo).

虛心, 'The Empty Heart.' But I fail to see the applicability of the title. The subject of the chapter is the Tâo in its operation. This is the significance of the 德 in the first clause or line, and to render it by 'virtue,' as Julien and Chalmers do, only serves to hide the meaning. Julien, however, says that 'the virtue is that of the Tâo; and he is right in taking 從, the last character of the second line, as having the sense of 'from,' 'the source from,' and not, as Chalmers does, in the sense of 'following.'

Lâo-dze's mind is occupied with a very difficult subject to describe the production of material forms by the Tâo; how or from what, he does not say. What I have rendered 'semblances,' Julien 'les images,' and Chalmers 'forms,' seems, as the latter says, in some way to correspond to the 'Eternal Ideas' of Plato in the Divine Mind. But Lâo-dze had no idea of 'personality' in the Tâo.

22

22. 1. The partial becomes complete; the crooked, straight; the empty, full; the worn out, new. He whose (desires) are few gets them; he whose (desires) are many goes astray.

2. Therefore the sage holds in his embrace the one thing (of humility), and manifests it to all the world. He is free from self-display, and therefore he shines; from self-assertion, and therefore he is distinguished; from self-boasting, and therefore his merit is acknowledged; from self-complacency, and therefore he acquires superiority. It is because he is thus free from striving that therefore no one in the world is able to strive with him.

3. That saying of the ancients that 'the partial becomes complete' was not vainly spoken:–all real completion is comprehended under it.

益謙, 'The Increase granted to Humility.' This title rightly expresses the subject-matter of the chapter. I cannot translate the first clause otherwise than I have done. It was an old saying, which Lâo-dze found and adopted. Whether it was intended to embrace all the cases which are mentioned may be questioned, but he employs it so as to make it do so.

'The emptiness' which becomes full is literally the hollowness of a cavity in the ground which is sure to be filled by overflowing water;–see Mencius, IV, ii, 18. 'The worn out' is explained by the withered foliage of a tree, which comes out new and fresh in the next spring. I have taken the first sentence of par. 2 as Wû Khäng does;–see his commentary.

23

23. 1. Abstaining from speech marks him who is obeying the spontaneity of his nature. A violent wind does not last for a whole morning; a sudden rain does not last for the whole day. To whom is it that these (two) things are owing? To Heaven and Earth. If Heaven and Earth cannot make such (spasmodic) actings last long, how much less can man!

2. Therefore when one is making the Tâo his business, those who are also pursuing it, agree with him in it, and those who are making the manifestation of its course their object agree with him in that; while even those who are failing in both these things agree with him where they fail.

3. Hence, those with whom he agrees as to the Tâo have the happiness of attaining to it; those with whom he agrees as to its manifestation have the happiness of attaining to it; and those with whom he agrees in their failure have also the happiness of attaining (to the Tâo). (But) when there is not faith sufficient (on his part), a want of faith (in him) ensues (on the part of the others).

虛無, 'Absolute Vacancy.' This, I think, is the meaning of the title, 'Emptiness and Nothingness,' an entire conformity to the Tâo in him who professes to be directed by it. Such a one will be omnipotent in his influence in all others. The Tâo in him will restrain all (spasmodic) loquacity. Those who are described in par. 2 as 'failing' are not to be thought of as bad men, men given up, as Julien has it, au crime. They are simply ordinary men, who have failed in their study of the Tâo and practice of it, but are won to truth and virtue by the man whom the author has in mind. As we might expect, however, the mention of such men has much embarrassed the commentators.

Compare the concluding sentence with the one at the end of par. 1 in Ch. 17.

24

24. He who stands on his tiptoes does not stand firm; he who stretches his legs does not walk (easily). (So), he who displays himself does not shine; he who asserts his own views is not distinguished; he who vaunts himself does not find his merit acknowledged; he who is self-conceited has no superiority allowed to him. Such conditions, viewed from the standpoint of the Tâo, are like remnants of food, or a tumour on the body, which all dislike. Hence those who pursue (the course) of the Tâo do not adopt and allow them.

苦恩, 'Painful Graciousness.' The chapter should be so designated. This concludes the subject of the two previous chapters,pursuing the course, the course of the unemotional Tâo without vain effort or display.

The remnants of food were not used as sacrificial offerings;–see the Lî Kî (vol. xxvii, p. 82). In what I have rendered by 'a tumour attached to the body,' the 行 is probably, by a mistake, for 形;–see a quotation by Wû Khäng from Sze-mâ Khien. "Which all dislike' is, literally, 'Things are likely to dislike them,' the 'things' being 'spirits and men,' as Wû explains the term.

25

25. 1. There was something undefined and complete, coming into existence before Heaven and Earth. How still it was and formless, standing alone, and undergoing no change, reaching everywhere and in no danger (of being exhausted)! It may be regarded as the Mother of all things.

2. I do not know its name, and I give it the designation of the Tâo (the Way or Course). Making an effort (further) to give it a name I call it The Great.

3. Great, it passes on (in constant flow). Passing on, it becomes remote. Having become remote, it returns. Therefore the Tâo is great; Heaven is great; Earth is great; and the (sage) king is also great. In the universe there are four that are great, and the (sage) king is one of them.

4. Man takes his law from the Earth; the Earth takes its law from Heaven; Heaven takes its law from the Tâo. The law of the Tâo is its being what it is.

象玄, 'Representations of the Mystery.' In this chapter Lâo approaches very near to give an answer to the question as to what the Tâo is, and yet leaves the reader disappointed. He commences by calling it 'a thing (物);' but that term does not necessitate our regarding it as 'material'! We have seen in the preceding chapter that it is used to signify 'spirits and men.' Nor does his going on to speak of it as 'chaotic' (混成) I necessarily lead us to conceive it as made up of the 'material elements of things;' we have the same term applied in Ch. 14 to the three immaterial constituents there said to be blended in the idea of it.

'He does not know its name,' and he designates it by the term denoting a course or way (Tâo, 道), and indicating the phenomenal attribute, the method in which all phenomena come before our observation, in their development or evolution. And to distinguish it from all other methods of evolution, he would call it 'the Great Method,' and so he employs that combination as its name in Ch. 18 and elsewhere; but it cannot be said that this name has fully maintained itself in the writings of his followers. But understood thus, he here says, as in Ch. 1, that it is 'the Mother of all things.' And yet, when he says that 'it was before Heaven and Earth were produced,' he comes very near his affirmations in chapters 1 and 4, that 'the nameless Tâo was the beginning (or originating cause) of Heaven and Earth,' and 'might seem to have been before God.' Was he groping after God if haply he might find Him? I think he was, and he gets so far as to conceive of Him as 'the Uncaused Cause,' but comes short of the idea of His personality. The other subordinate causes which he mentions all get their force or power from the Tâo, but after all the Tâo is simply a spontaneity, evolving from itself, and not acting from a personal will, consciously in the direction of its own wisdom and love. 'Who can by searching find out God? Who can find out the Almighty to perfection?'

The predicate of the Tâo in the chapter, most perplexing to myself, is 'It returns,' in par. 3. 'It flows away, far away, and comes back;'–are not the three statements together equal to 'It is everywhere?'

26

26. 1. Gravity is the root of lightness; stillness, the ruler of movement.

2. Therefore a wise prince, marching the whole day, does not go far from his baggage waggons. Although he may have brilliant prospects to look at, he quietly remains (in his proper place), indifferent to them. How should the lord of a myriad chariots carry himself lightly before the kingdom? If he do act lightly, he has lost his root (of gravity); if he proceed to active movement, he will lose his throne.

重德, 'The Quality of Gravity.' Gravity and stillness are both attributes of the Tâo; and he who cultivates it must not give way to lightness of mind, or hasty action.

The rule for a leader not to separate from his baggage waggons is simply the necessity of adhering to gravity. I have adopted from Han Fei the reading of 'the wise prince' for 'the sage,' which is found in Ho-shang Kung; and later on the reading of 'has lost his root' for his 'loses his ministers,' though the latter is found also in Han Fei.

27

27. 1. The skilful traveller leaves no traces of his wheels or footsteps; the skilful speaker says nothing that can be found fault with or blamed; the skilful reckoner uses no tallies; the skilful closer needs no bolts or bars, while to open what he has shut will be impossible; the skilful binder uses no strings or knots, while to unloose what he has bound will be impossible. In the same way the sage is always skilful at saving men, and so he does not cast away any man; he is always skilful at saving things, and so he does not cast away anything. This is called 'Hiding the light of his procedure.'

2. Therefore the man of skill is a master (to be looked up to) by him who has not the skill; and he who has not the skill is the helper of (the reputation of) him who has the skill. If the one did not honour his master, and the other did not rejoice in his helper, an (observer), though intelligent, might greatly err about them. This is called 'The utmost degree of mystery.'

巧用, 'Dexterity in Using,' that is, in the application of the Tâo. This is the substance of the chapter, celebrating the effective but invisible operation of the Tâo, and the impartial exercise of it for the benefit of all men and all things.

I have given the most natural construction of the two characters at the end of par. 1, the only possible construction of them, so far as I can see, suitable to the context. The action of the Tâo (non-acting and yet all-efficient) and that of the sage in accordance with it, are veiled by their nature from the sight of ordinary men.

It is more difficult to catch the scope and point of par. 2. If there were not the conditions described in it, it would be hard for even an intelligent onlooker to distinguish between the man who had the skill and the man without it, between him who possessed the Tâo, and him who had it not, which would be strange indeed.

28

28. 1. Who knows his manhood's strength, Yet still his female feebleness maintains; As to one channel flow the many drains, All come to him, yea, all beneath the sky. Thus he the constant excellence retains; The simple child again, free from all stains.

Who knows how white attracts, Yet always keeps himself within black's shade, The pattern of humility displayed, Displayed in view of all beneath the sky; He in the unchanging excellence arrayed, Endless return to man's first state has made.

Who knows how glory shines, Yet loves disgrace, nor e'er for it is pale; Behold his presence in a spacious vale, To which men come from all beneath the sky. The unchanging excellence completes its tale; The simple infant man in him we hail.

2. The unwrought material, when divided and distributed, forms vessels. The sage, when employed, becomes the Head of all the Officers (of government); and in his greatest regulations he employs no violent measures.

反樸, 'Returning to Simplicity.' The chapter sets forth humility and simplicity, an artless freedom from all purpose, as characteristic of the man of Tâo, such as he was in the primeval time. 'The sage' in par. 2 may be 'the Son of Heaven,'–the Head of all rule in the kingdom, or the feudal lord in a state.

29

29. 1. If any one should wish to get the kingdom for himself, and to effect this by what he does, I see that he will not succeed. The kingdom is a spirit-like thing, and cannot be got by active doing. He who would so win it destroys it; he who would hold it in his grasp loses it.

2. The course and nature of things is such that What was in front is now behind; What warmed anon we freezing find. Strength is of weakness oft the spoil; The store in ruins mocks our toil.

Hence the sage puts away excessive effort, extravagance, and easy indulgence.

無爲, 'Taking no Action.' All efforts made with a purpose are sure to fail. The nature of the Tâo necessitates their doing so, and the uncertainty of things and events teaches the same lesson.

That the kingdom or throne is a 'spirit-like vessel' has become a common enough saying among the Chinese. Julien has, 'L'Empire est comme un vase divin;' but I always shrink from translating 神 by 'divine.' Its English analogue is 'spirit,' and the idea in the text is based on the immunity of spirit from all material law, and the uncertain issue of attempts to deal with it according to ordinary methods. Wû Khäng takes the phrase as equivalent to 'superintended by spirits,' which is as inadmissible as Julien's 'divin.' The Tâo forbids action with a personal purpose, and all such action is sure to fail in the greatest things as well as in the least.

30

30. 1. He who would assist a lord of men in harmony with the Tâo will not assert his mastery in the kingdom by force of arms. Such a course is sure to meet with its proper return.

2. Wherever a host is stationed, briars and thorns spring up. In the sequence of great armies there are sure to be bad years.

3. A skilful (commander) strikes a decisive blow, and stops. He does not dare (by continuing his operations) to assert and complete his mastery. He will strike the blow, but will be on his guard against being vain or boastful or arrogant in consequence of it. He strikes it as a matter of necessity; he strikes it, but not from a wish for mastery.

4. When things have attained their strong maturity they become old. This may be said to be not in accordance with the Tâo: and what is not in accordance with it soon comes to an end.

儉武, 'A Caveat against War.' War is contrary to the spirit of the Tâo, and, as being so, is productive of misery, and leads to early ruin. It is only permissible in a case of necessity, and even then its spirit and tendencies must be guarded against.

In translating 果 by 'striking a decisive blow,' I have, no doubt, followed Julien's 'frapper un coup décisif.' The same; 果 occurs six times in par. 3, followed by 而, and Ziâo Hung says that in all but the first instance the 而 should be taken as equivalent to 於, so that we should have to translate, 'He is determined against being vain,' &c. But there is no necessity for such a construction of 而.

'Weakness' and not 'strength' is the character of the Tâo; hence the lesson in par. 4.

31

31. 1. Now arms, however beautiful, are instruments of evil omen, hateful, it may be said, to all creatures. Therefore they who have the Tâo do not like to employ them.

2. The superior man ordinarily considers the left hand the most honourable place, but in time of war the right hand. Those sharp weapons are instruments of evil omen, and not the instruments of the superior man;–he uses them only on the compulsion of necessity. Calm and repose are what he prizes; victory (by force of arms) is to him undesirable. To consider this desirable would be to delight in the slaughter of men; and he who delights in the slaughter of men cannot get his will in the kingdom.

3. On occasions of festivity to be on the left hand is the prized position; on occasions of mourning, the right hand. The second in command of the army has his place on the left; the general commanding in chief has his on the right;–his place, that is, is assigned to him as in the rites of mourning. He who has killed multitudes of men should weep for them with the bitterest grief; and the victor in battle has his place (rightly) according to those rites.

偃武, 'Stilling War.' The chapter continues the subject of the preceding. The imperially-appointed editors of Wang Pî's Text and Commentary (1765) say that from the beginning of par. 2 to the end, there is the appearance of text and commentary being mixed together; but they make no alteration in the text as it is found in Ho-shang Kung, and in all other ancient copies.

The concluding sentence will suggest to some readers the words of the Duke of Wellington, that to gain a battle was the saddest thing next to losing it.

32

32. 1. The Tâo, considered as unchanging, has no name.

2. Though in its primordial simplicity it may be small, the whole world dares not deal with (one embodying) it as a minister. If a feudal prince or the king could guard and hold it, all would spontaneously submit themselves to him.

3. Heaven and Earth (under its guidance) unite together and send down the sweet dew, which, without the directions of men, reaches equally everywhere as of its own accord.

4. As soon as it proceeds to action, it has a name. When it once has that name, (men) can know to rest in it. When they know to rest in it, they can be free from all risk of failure and error.

5. The relation of the Tâo to all the world is like that of the great rivers and seas to the streams from the valleys.

聖 德, Chalmers translates this by "sagely virtue." But I cannot adopt that rendering, and find it difficult to supply a better. The 'virtue' is evidently the Attribute of the Tâo come out from the condition of the Absolute, and capable of being named. In the former state it has no name; in the latter, it has. Par. 1 and the commencement of par. 4 must both be explained from Ch. 1.

The 'primordial simplicity' in par. 2 is the Tâo in its simplest conception, alone, and by itself, and the **始 制** in par. 4 is that Tâo come forth into operation and become Teh, the Teh which affords a law for men. From this to the end of the paragraph is very obscure. I have translated from the text of Wang Pî. The text of Ho-shang Kung is different, and he comments upon it as it stands, but to me it is inexplicable.

33

33. 1. He who knows other men is discerning; he who knows himself is intelligent. He who overcomes others is strong; he who overcomes himself is mighty. He who is satisfied with his lot is rich; he who goes on acting with energy has a (firm) will.

2. He who does not fail in the requirements of his position, continues long; he who dies and yet does not perish, has longevity.

辨德, 'Discriminating between (different) Attributes.' The teaching of the chapter is that the possession of the Tâo confers the various attributes which are here most distinguished. It has been objected to it that elsewhere the Tâo is represented as associated with dullness and not intelligence, and with weakness and not with strength. But these seem to be qualities viewed from without, and acting on what is beyond itself. Inwardly, its qualities are the very opposite, and its action has the effect of enlightening what is dark, and overcoming what is strong.

More interesting are the predicates in par. 2. Ziâo Hung gives the comment on it of the Indian monk, Kumâragîva, 'one of the four suns of Buddhism, and who went to China in A.D. 401': 'To be alive and yet not alive may well be called long; to die and yet not be dead may well be called longevity.' He also gives the views of Lû Näng-shih (A.D. 1042-1102) that the freedom from change of Lieh-dze, from death of Kwang-dze, and from extinction of the Buddhists, have all the same meaning as the concluding saying of Lâo-dze here; that the human body is like the covering of the caterpillar or the skin of the snake; that we occupy it but for a passing sojourn. No doubt, Lâo-dze believed in another life for the individual after the present. Many passages in Kwang-dze indicate the same faith.

34

34. 1. All-pervading is the Great Tâo! It may be found on the left hand and on the right.

2. All things depend on it for their production, which it gives to them, not one refusing obedience to it. When its work is accomplished, it does not claim the name of having done it. It clothes all things as with a garment, and makes no assumption of being their lord;–it may be named in the smallest things. All things return (to their root and disappear), and do not know that it is it which presides over their doing so;–it may be named in the greatest things.

3. Hence the sage is able (in the same way) to accomplish his great achievements. It is through his not making himself great that he can accomplish them.

任成, 'The Task of Achievement!' The subject is the greatness of what the Tâo, called here by Lâo's own name for it in Ch. 25, does; and the unconscious simplicity with which it does it; and then the achievements of the sage who is permeated by the Tâo. Par. 2 is descriptive of the influence of the Tâo in the vegetable world. The statements and expressions are much akin to those in parts of chapters 2, 10, and 51, and for Ho-shang Kung's difficult reading of 不名有 some copies give 仁德, as in Ch. 2.

35

35. 1. To him who holds in his hands the Great Image (of the invisible Tâo), the whole world repairs. Men resort to him, and receive no hurt, but (find) rest, peace, and the feeling of ease.

2. Music and dainties will make the passing guest stop (for a time). But though the Tâo as it comes from the mouth, seems insipid and has no flavour, though it seems not worth being looked at or listened to, the use of it is inexhaustible.

仁德 'The Attribute of Benevolence.' But there seems little appropriateness in this title. The subject of the chapter is the inexhaustible efficacy of the Tâo for the good of the world.

The Great Image (of the invisible Tâo) is a name for the Tâo, in its operation; as in chapters 14 and 41. He who embodies this in his government will be a centre of attraction for all the world. Or the 天下往 may be taken as a predicate of the holder of the Great Image:–'If he go all under heaven teaching the Tâo.' Both constructions are maintained by commentators of note. In par. 2 the attraction of the Tâo is contrasted with that of ordinary pleasures and gratifications.

36

36. 1. When one is about to take an inspiration, he is sure to make a (previous) expiration; when he is going to weaken another, he will first strengthen him; when he is going to overthrow another, he will first have raised him up; when he is going to despoil another, he will first have made gifts to him:– this is called 'Hiding the light (of his procedure).'

2. The soft overcomes the hard; and the weak the strong.

3. Fishes should not be taken from the deep; instruments for the profit of a state should not be shown to the people.

微明, 'Minimising the Light;' equivalent, as Wû Khäng has pointed out, to the 襲明 of Ch. 27.

The gist of the chapter is to be sought in the second paragraph, where we have two instances of the action of the Tâo by contraries, supposed always to be for good.

But there is a difficulty in seeing the applicability to this of the cases mentioned in par. 1. The first case, indeed, is merely a natural phenomenon, having no moral character; but the others, as they have been illustrated from historical incidents, by Han Fei and others at least, belong to schemes of selfish and unprincipled ambitious strategy, which it would be injurious to Lâo-dze to suppose that he intended.

Par. 3 is the most frequently quoted of all the passages in our King, unless it be the first part of Ch. 1. Fishes taken from the deep, and brought into shallow water, can be easily taken or killed; that is plain enough. 'The sharp instruments of a state' are not its 'weapons of war,' nor its 'treasures,' nor its 'instruments of government,' that is, its rewards and punishments, though this last is the interpretation often put on them, and sustained by a foolish reference to an incident, real or coined, in the history of the dukedom of Sung. The lî khî are 'contrivances for gain,' machines, and other methods to increase the wealth of a state, but, according to the principles of Lâo-dze, really injurious to it. These should not be shown to the people, whom the Tâoistic system would keep in a state of primitive simplicity and ignorance. This interpretation is in accordance with the meaning of the characters, and with the general teaching of Tâoism. In no other way can I explain the paragraph so as to justify the place undoubtedly belonging to it in the system.

37

37. 1. The Tâo in its regular course does nothing (for the sake of doing it), and so there is nothing which it does not do.

2. If princes and kings were able to maintain it, all things would of themselves be transformed by them.

3. If this transformation became to me an object of desire, I would express the desire by the nameless simplicity.

Simplicity without a name Is free from all external aim. With no desire, at rest and still, All things go right as of their will.

爲政, 'The Exercise of Government.' This exercise should be according to the Tâo, doing without doing, governing without government.

The subject of the third paragraph is a feudal prince or the king, and he is spoken of in the first person, to give more vividness to the style, unless the 吾, 'I,' may, possibly, be understood of Lâo-dze himself personating one of them.

PART II

38

38. 1. (Those who) possessed in highest degree the attributes (of the Tâo) did not (seek) to show them, and therefore they possessed them (in fullest measure). (Those who) possessed in a lower degree those attributes (sought how) not to lose them, and therefore they did not possess them (in fullest measure).

2. (Those who) possessed in the highest degree those attributes did nothing (with a purpose), and had no need to do anything. (Those who) possessed them in a lower degree were (always) doing, and had need to be so doing.

3. (Those who) possessed the highest benevolence were (always seeking) to carry it out, and had no need to be doing so. (Those who) possessed the highest righteousness were (always seeking) to carry it out, and had need to be so doing.

4. (Those who) possessed the highest (sense of) propriety were (always seeking) to show it, and when men did not respond to it, they bared the arm and marched up to them.

5. Thus it was that when the Tâo was lost, its attributes appeared; when its attributes were lost, benevolence appeared; when benevolence was lost, righteousness appeared; and when righteousness was lost, the proprieties appeared.

6. Now propriety is the attenuated form of leal-heartedness and good faith, and is also the commencement of disorder; swift apprehension is (only) a flower of the Tâo, and is the beginning of stupidity.

7. Thus it is that the Great man abides by what is solid, and eschews what is flimsy; dwells with the fruit and not with the flower. It is thus that he puts away the one and makes choice of the other.

論德, 'About the Attributes;' of Tâo, that is. It is not easy to render teh here by any other English term than 'virtue,' and yet there would be a danger of its thus misleading us in the interpretation of the chapter.

The 'virtue' is the activity or operation of the Tâo, which is supposed to have come out of its absoluteness. Even Han Fei so defines it here,–'Teh is the meritorious work of the Tâo.'

In par. 5 we evidently have a résumé of the preceding paragraphs, and, as it is historical, I translate them in the past tense; though what took place on the early stage of the world may also be said to go on taking place in the experience of every individual. With some considerable hesitation I have given the subjects in those paragraphs in the concrete, in deference to the authority of Ho-shang Kung and most other commentators. The former says, 'By "the highest teh" is to be understood the rulers of the greatest antiquity, without name or designation, whose virtue was great, and could not be surpassed.' Most ingenious, and in accordance with the Tâoistic system, is the manner in which Wû Khăng construes the passage, and I am surprised that it has not been generally accepted. By 'the higher teh' he understands 'the Tâo,' that which is prior to and above the Teh (上德者, 在德之上道也) by 'the lower teh,' benevolence, that which is after and below the Teh; by 'the higher benevolence,' the Teh which is above benevolence; by 'the higher righteousness,' the benevolence which is above righteousness; and by 'the higher propriety,' the righteousness which is above propriety. Certainly in the summation of these four paragraphs which we have in the fifth, the subjects of them would appear to have been in the mind of Lâo-dze as thus defined by Wû.

In the remainder of the chapter he goes on to speak depreciatingly of ceremonies and knowledge, so that the whole chapter must be understood as descriptive of the process of decay and deterioration from the early time in which the Tâo and its attributes swayed the societies of men.

39

39. 1. The things which from of old have got the One (the Tâo) are–

Heaven which by it is bright and pure; Earth rendered thereby firm and sure; Spirits with powers by it supplied; Valleys kept full throughout their void All creatures which through it do live Princes and kings who from it get The model which to all they give. All these are the results of the One (Tâo).

2. If heaven were not thus pure, it soon would rend; If earth were not thus sure, 'twould break and bend; Without these powers, the spirits soon would fail; If not so filled, the drought would parch each vale; Without that life, creatures would pass away; Princes and kings, without that moral sway, However grand and high, would all decay.

3. Thus it is that dignity finds its (firm) root in its (previous) meanness, and what is lofty finds its stability in the lowness (from which it rises). Hence princes and kings call themselves 'Orphans,' 'Men of small virtue,' and as 'Carriages without a nave.' Is not this an acknowledgment that in their considering themselves mean they see the foundation of their dignity? So it is that in the enumeration of the different parts of a carriage we do not come on what makes it answer the ends of a carriage. They do not wish to show themselves elegant-looking as jade, but (prefer) to be coarse-looking as an (ordinary) stone.

法本, 'The Origin of the Law.' In this title there is a reference to the Law given to all things by the Tâo, as described in the conclusion of

Ch. 25. And the Tâo affords that law by its passionless, undemonstrative nature, through which in its spontaneity, doing nothing for the sake of doing, it yet does all things.

The difficulty of translation is in the third paragraph. The way in which princes and kings speak depreciatingly of themselves is adduced as illustrating how they have indeed got the spirit of the Tâo; and I accept the last epithet as given by Ho-shang Kung, 'naveless' (轂), instead of 穀 (='the unworthy'), which is found in Wang Pî, and has been adopted by nearly all subsequent editors. To see its appropriateness here, we have only to refer back to Ch. 11, where the thirty spokes, and the nave, empty to receive the axle, are spoken of, and it is shown how the usefulness of the carriage is derived from that emptiness of the nave. This also enables us to give a fair and consistent explanation of the difficult clause which follows, in which also I have followed the text of Ho-shang Kung. For his 車, Wang Pî has 輿, which also is found in a quotation of it by Hwâi-nan Dze; but this need not affect the meaning. In the translation of the clause we are assisted by a somewhat similar illustration about a horse in the twenty-fifth of Kwang-dze's Books, par. 10.

40

40. 1. The movement of the Tâo by contraries proceeds; And weakness marks the course of Tâo's mighty deeds.

2. All things under heaven sprang from It as existing (and named); that existence sprang from It as non-existent (and not named).

去用, 'Dispensing with the Use (of Means);'–with their use, that is, as it appears to us. The subject of the brief chapter is the action of the Tâo by contraries, leading to a result the opposite of what existed previously, and by means which might seem calculated to produce a contrary result.

In translating par. 2 I have followed Ziâo Hung, who finds the key to it in Ch. 1. Having a name, the Tâo is 'the Mother of all things;' having no name, it is 'the Originator of Heaven and Earth.' But here is the teaching of Lâo-dze:–'If Tâo seems to be before God,' Tâo itself sprang from nothing.

41

41. 1. Scholars of the highest class, when they hear about the Tâo, earnestly carry it into practice. Scholars of the middle class, when they have heard about it, seem now to keep it and now to lose it. Scholars of the lowest class, when they have heard about it, laugh greatly at it. If it were not (thus) laughed at, it would not be fit to be the Tâo.

2. Therefore the sentence-makers have thus expressed themselves:–

'The Tâo, when brightest seen, seems light to lack; Who progress in it makes, seems drawing back; Its even way is like a rugged track. Its highest virtue from the vale doth rise; Its greatest beauty seems to offend the eyes And he has most whose lot the least supplies. Its firmest virtue seems but poor and low; Its solid truth seems change to undergo; Its largest square doth yet no corner show A vessel great, it is the slowest made; Loud is its sound, but never word it said; A semblance great, the shadow of a shade.'

3. The Tâo is hidden, and has no name; but it is the Tâo which is skilful at imparting (to all things what they need) and making them complete.

同 異, 'Sameness and Difference.' The chapter is a sequel of the preceding, and may be taken as an illustration of the Tâo's proceeding by contraries.

Who the sentence-makers were whose sayings are quoted we cannot tell, but it would have been strange if Lâo-dze had not had a large store of such sentences at his command. The fifth and sixth of those employed by him here are found in Lieh-dze (II, 15 a), spoken by Lâo in reproving Yang Kû, and in VII, 3 a, that heretic appears quoting an utterance of the same kind, with the words,' according to an old saying (古語有之)'.

42

42\. 1. The Tâo produced One; One produced Two; Two produced Three; Three produced All things. All things leave behind them the Obscurity (out of which they have come), and go forward to embrace the Brightness (into which they have emerged), while they are harmonised by the Breath of Vacancy.

2\. What men dislike is to be orphans, to have little virtue, to be as carriages without naves; and yet these are the designations which kings and princes use for themselves. So it is that some things are increased by being diminished, and others are diminished by being increased.

3\. What other men (thus) teach, I also teach. The violent and strong do not die their natural death. I will make this the basis of my teaching.

道化, 'The Transformations of the Tâo.' In par. 2 we have the case of the depreciating epithets given to themselves by kings and princes, which we found before in Ch. 39, and a similar lesson is drawn from it. Such depreciation leads to exaltation, and the contrary course of self-exaltation leads to abasement. This latter case is stated emphatically in par. 3, and Lâo-dze says that it was the basis of his teaching. So far therefore we have in this chapter a repetition of the lesson that the movement of the Tâo is by contraries, and that its weakness is the sure precursor of strength. But the connexion between this lesson and what he says in par. 1 it is difficult to trace. Up to this time at least it has baffled myself. The passage seems to give us a cosmogony. 'The Tâo produced One.' We have already seen that the Tâo is 'The One.' Are we to understand here that the Tâo, and the One were one and the same?

In this case what would be the significance of the 生 ('produced')?– that the Tâo which had been previously 'non-existent' now became 'existent,' or capable of being named? This seems to be the view of Szemâ Kwang (A.D. 1009-1086).

The most singular form which this view assumes is in one of the treatises on our King, attributed to the Tâoist patriarch Lü (呂祖道德經解), that 'the One is Heaven, which was formed by the congealing of the Tâo.' According to another treatise, also assigned to the same Lü (道德眞經合解) the One was 'the primordial ether;' the Two, 'the separation of that into its Yin and Yang constituents;' and the Three, 'the production of heaven, earth, and man by these.' In quoting the paragraph Hwâi-nan dze omits 道生一, and commences with 一生二, and his glossarist, Kâo Yû, makes out the One to be the Tâo, the Two to be Spiritual Intelligences (神明), and the Three to be the Harmonising Breath. From the mention of the Yin and Yang that follows, I believe that Lâo-dze intended by the Two these two qualities or elements in the primordial ether, which would be 'the One.' I dare not hazard a guess as to what 'the Three' were.

43

43. 1. The softest thing in the world dashes against and overcomes the hardest; that which has no (substantial) existence enters where there is no crevice. I know hereby what advantage belongs to doing nothing (with a purpose).

2. There are few in the world who attain to the teaching without words, and the advantage arising from non-action.

偏用, 'The Universal Use (of the action in weakness of the Tâo).' The chapter takes us back to the lines of Ch. 40, that 'Weakness marks the course of Tâo's mighty deeds.'

By 'the softest thing in the world' it is agreed that we are to understand 'water,' which will wear away the hardest rocks. 'Dashing against and overcoming' is a metaphor taken from hunting. Ho-shang Kung says that 'what has no existence' is the Tâo; it is better to understand by it the unsubstantial air (**氣**) which penetrates everywhere, we cannot see how.

Compare par. 2 with Ch. 2, par. 3.

44

44. 1. Or fame or life, Which do you hold more dear? Or life or wealth, To which would you adhere? Keep life and lose those other things; Keep them and lose your life:–which brings Sorrow and pain more near?

2. Thus we may see, Who cleaves to fame Rejects what is more great; Who loves large stores Gives up the richer state.

3. Who is content Needs fear no shame. Who knows to stop Incurs no blame. From danger free Long live shall he.

立戒, 'Cautions.' The chapter warns men to let nothing come into competition with the value which they set on the Tâo. The Tâo is not named, indeed, but the idea of it was evidently in the writer's mind.

The whole chapter rhymes after a somewhat peculiar fashion; familiar enough, however, to one who is acquainted with the old rhymes of the Book of Poetry.

45

45. 1. Who thinks his great achievements poor Shall find his vigour long endure. Of greatest fullness, deemed a void, Exhaustion ne'er shall stem the tide. Do thou what's straight still crooked deem; Thy greatest art still stupid seem, And eloquence a stammering scream.

2. Constant action overcomes cold; being still overcomes heat. Purity and stillness give the correct law to all under heaven.

洪德, 'Great or Overflowing Virtue.' The chapter is another illustration of the working of the Tâo by contraries. According to Wû Khäng, the action which overcomes cold is that of the Yang element in the developing primordial ether; and the stillness which overcomes heat is that of the contrary Yin element. These may have been in Lâo-dze's mind, but the statements are so simple as hardly to need any comment. Wû further says that the purity and stillness are descriptive of the condition of non-action.

46

46. 1. When the Tâo prevails in the world, they send back their swift horses to (draw) the dung-carts.

When the Tâo is disregarded in the world, the war-horses breed in the border lands.

2. There is no guilt greater than to sanction ambition; no calamity greater than to be discontented with one's lot; no fault greater than the wish to be getting. Therefore the sufficiency of contentment is an enduring and unchanging sufficiency.

儉欲, 'The Moderating of Desire or Ambition.' The chapter shows how the practice of the Tâo must conduce to contentment and happiness.

In translating par. 1 I have, after Wû Khäng, admitted a 車 after the 糞, his chief authority for doing so being that it is so found in a poetical piece by Kang Häng (A.D. 78-139). Kû Hsî also adopted this reading (朱子大全, XVIII, 7 a). In par. 2 Han Ying has a tempting variation of 多欲 for 可欲, but I have not adopted it because the same phrase occurs elsewhere.

47

47. 1. Without going outside his door, one understands (all that takes place) under the sky; without looking out from his window, one sees the Tâo of Heaven. The farther that one goes out (from himself), the less he knows.

2. Therefore the sages got their knowledge without travelling; gave their (right) names to things without seeing them; and accomplished their ends without any purpose of doing so.

鑒遠, 'Surveying what is Far-off.' The chapter is a lesson to men to judge of things according to their internal conviction of similar things in their own experience. Short as the chapter is, it is somewhat mystical. The phrase, 'The Tâo' or way of Heaven, occurs in it for the first time; and it is difficult to lay down its precise meaning. Lâo-dze would seem to teach that man is a microcosm; and that, if he understand the movements of his own mind, he can understand the movements of all other minds. There are various readings, of which it is not necessary to speak.

I have translated par. 2 in the past tense, and perhaps the first should also be translated so. Most of it is found in Han Ying, preceded by 'formerly' or 'anciently.'

48

48\. 1. He who devotes himself to learning (seeks) from day to day to increase (his knowledge); he who devotes himself to the Tâo (seeks) from day to day to diminish (his doing).

2\. He diminishes it and again diminishes it, till he arrives at doing nothing (on purpose). Having arrived at this point of non-action, there is nothing which he does not do.

3\. He who gets as his own all under heaven does so by giving himself no trouble (with that end). If one take trouble (with that end), he is not equal to getting as his own all under heaven.

忘知, 'Forgetting Knowledge;–he contrast between Learning and the Tâo. It is only by the Tâo that the world can be won.

Ziâo Hung commences his quotations of commentary on this chapter with the following from Kumâragîva on the second par.:–'He carries on the process of diminishing till there is nothing coarse about him which is not put away. He puts it away till he has forgotten all that was bad in it. He then puts away all that is fine about him. He does so till he has forgotten all that was good in it. But the bad was wrong, and the good is right. Having diminished the wrong, and also diminished the right, the process is carried on till they are both forgotten. Passion and desire are both cut off; and his virtue and the Tâo are in such union that he does nothing; but though he does nothing, he allows all things to do their own doing, and all things are done.' Such is a Buddhistic view of the passage, not very intelligible, and which I do not endorse.

In a passage in the 'Narratives of the School' (Bk. IX, Art. 2), we have a Confucian view of the passage:–'Let perspicacity, intelligence, shrewdness, and wisdom be guarded by stupidity, and the service of the possessor will affect the whole world; let them be guarded by complaisance, and his dating and strength will shake the age; let them be guarded by timidity, and his wealth will be all within the four seas; let them be guarded by humility, and there will be what we call the method of "diminishing it, and diminishing it again." But neither do I endorse this.

My own view of the scope of the chapter has been given above in a few words. The greater part of it is found in Kwang-dze.

49

49. 1. The sage has no invariable mind of his own; he makes the mind of the people his mind.

2. To those who are good (to me), I am good; and to those who are not good (to me), I am also good;–and thus (all) get to be good. To those who are sincere (with me), I am sincere; and to those who are not sincere (with me), I am also sincere;–and thus (all) get to be sincere.

3. The sage has in the world an appearance of indecision, and keeps his mind in a state of indifference to all. The people all keep their eyes and ears directed to him, and he deals with them all as his children.

任德, 'The Quality of Indulgence.' The chapter shows how that quality enters largely into the dealing of the sage with other men, and exercises over them a transforming influence, dominated as it is in him by the Tâo.

My version of par. 1 is taken from Dr. Chalmers. A good commentary on it was given by the last emperor but one of the earlier of the two great Sung dynasties, in the period A.D. 1111-1117:–'The mind of the sage is free from preoccupation and able to receive; still, and able to respond.'

In par. 2 I adopt the reading of to get 得 ('to get') instead of the more common 德 ('virtue' or 'quality'). There is a passage in Han Ying (IX, 3 b, 4 a), the style of which, most readers will probably agree with me in thinking, was moulded on the text before us, though nothing is said of any connexion between it and the saying of Lâo-dze. I must regard it as a sequel to the conversation between Confucius and some of his disciples about the principle (Lâo's principle) that 'Injury should be recompensed with Kindness,' as recorded in the Con. Ana., XIV, 36. We read:–'Dze-lû said, "When men are good to me, I will also be good to them; when they are not good to me, I will also be not good to them." Dze-kung said, "When men are good to me, I will also be good to them; when they are not good to me, I will simply lead them on, forwards it may be or backwards." Yen Hui said, "When men are good to me, I will also be good to them when they are not good to me, I will still be good to them." The views of the three disciples being thus different, they referred the point to the Master, who said, "The words of Dze-lû are such as might be expected among the (wild tribes of) the Man and the Mo; those of Dze-kung, such as might be expected among friends; those of Hui, such as might be expected among relatives and near connexions." This is all. The Master was still far from Lâo-dze's standpoint, and that of his own favourite disciple, Yen Hui.

50

50. 1. Men come forth and live; they enter (again) and die.

2. Of every ten three are ministers of life (to themselves); and three are ministers of death.

3. There are also three in every ten whose aim is to live, but whose movements tend to the land (or place) of death. And for what reason? Because of their excessive endeavours to perpetuate life.

4. But I have heard that he who is skilful in managing the life entrusted to him for a time travels on the land without having to shun rhinoceros or tiger, and enters a host without having to avoid buff coat or sharp weapon. The rhinoceros finds no place in him into which to thrust its horn, nor the tiger a place in which to fix its claws, nor the weapon a place to admit its point. And for what reason? Because there is in him no place of death.

貴生, 'The Value set on Life.' The chapter sets forth the Tâo as an antidote against decay and death.

In par. 1 life is presented to us as intermediate between two non-existences. The words will suggest to many readers those in Job i. 21.

In pars. 2 and 3 I translate the characters 十有三 by 'three in ten,' instead of by 'thirteen,' as Julien and other translators have done. The characters are susceptible of either translation according to the tone in which we read the 有. They were construed as I have done by Wang Pî; and many of the best commentators have followed in his wake. 'The ministers of life to themselves' would be those who eschewed all things, both internal and external, tending to injure health; 'the ministers of death,' those who pursued courses likely to cause disease and shorten life; the third three would be those who thought that by mysterious and abnormal courses they could prolong life, but only injured it. Those three classes being thus disposed of, there remains only one in ten rightly using the Tâo, and he is spoken of in the next paragraph.

This par. 4 is easy of translation, and the various readings in it are unimportant, differing in this respect from those in par. 3. But the aim of the author in it is not clear. In ascribing such effects to the possession of the Tâo, is he 'trifling,' as Dr. Chalmers thinks? or indulging the play of his poetical fancy? or simply saying that the Tâoist will keep himself out of danger?

51

51. 1. All things are produced by the Tâo, and nourished by its outflowing operation. They receive their forms according to the nature of each, and are completed according to the circumstances of their condition. Therefore all things without exception honour the Tâo, and exalt its outflowing operation.

2. This honouring of the Tâo and exalting of its operation is not the result of any ordination, but always a spontaneous tribute.

3. Thus it is that the Tâo produces (all things), nourishes them, brings them to their full growth, nurses them, completes them, matures them, maintains them, and overspreads them.

4. It produces them and makes no claim to the possession of them; it carries them through their processes and does not vaunt its ability in doing so; it brings them to maturity and exercises no control over them;-this is called its mysterious operation.

養德, 'The Operation (of the Tâo) in Nourishing Things.' The subject of the chapter is the quiet passionless operation of the Tâo in nature, in the production and nourishing of things throughout the seasons of the year; a theme dwelt on by Lâo-dze, in II, 4, X, 3, and other places.

The Tâo is the subject of all the predicates in par. 1, and what seem the subjects in all but the first member should be construed adverbially.

On par. 2 Wû Khäng says that the honour of the Son of Heaven is derived from his appointment by God, and that then the nobility of the feudal princes is derived from him; but in the honour given to the

Tâo and the nobility ascribed to its operation, we are not to think of any external ordination. There is a strange reading of two of the members of par. 3 in Wang Pî, viz. 亭之毒之 for 成之熟之. This is quoted and predicated of 'Heaven,' in the Nestorian Monument of Hsî-an in the eighth century.

52

52. 1. (The Tâo) which originated all under the sky is to be considered as the mother of them all.

2. When the mother is found, we know what her children should be. When one knows that he is his mother's child, and proceeds to guard (the qualities of) the mother that belong to him, to the end of his life he will be free from all peril.

3. Let him keep his mouth closed, and shut up the portals (of his nostrils), and all his life he will be exempt from laborious exertion. Let him keep his mouth open, and (spend his breath) in the promotion of his affairs, and all his life there will be no safety for him.

4. The perception of what is small is (the secret of) clear-sightedness; the guarding of what is soft and tender is (the secret of) strength.

5. Who uses well his light, Reverting to its (source so) bright, Will from his body ward all blight, And hides the unchanging from men's sight.

歸元, 'Returning to the Source.' The meaning of the chapter is obscure, and the commentators give little help in determining it. As in the preceding chapter, Lâo-dze treats of the operation of the Tâo on material things, he seems in this to go on to the operation of it in man, or how he, with his higher nature, should ever be maintaining it in himself.

For the understanding of par. 1 we must refer to the first chapter of the treatise, where the Tâo, 'having no name,' appears as 'the Beginning' or 'First Cause' of the world, and then, 'having a name,' as its 'Mother.' It is the same thing or concept in both of its phases, the ideal or absolute, and the manifestation of it in its passionless doings. The old Jesuit translators render this paragraph by 'Mundus principium et causam suam habet in Divino 有, seu actione Divinae sapientiae quae dici potest ejus mater.' So far I may assume that they agreed with me in understanding that the subject of the paragraph was the Tâo.

Par. 2 lays down the law of life for man thus derived from the Tâo. The last clause of it is given by the same translators as equivalent to 'Unde fit ut post mortem nihil ei timendum sit,'–a meaning which the characters will not bear. But from that clause, and the next par., I am obliged to conclude that even in Lâo-dze's mind there was the germ of the sublimation of the material frame which issued in the asceticism and life-preserving arts of the later Tâoism.

Par. 3 seems to indicate the method of 'guarding the mother in man,' by watching over the breath, the proto-plastic 'one' of Ch. 42, the ethereal matter out of which all material things were formed. The organs of this breath in man are the mouth and nostrils (nothing else should be understood here by 兌 and 門;–see the explanations of the former in the last paragraph of the fifth of the appendixes to the Yî in vol. xvi, p. 432); and the management of the breath is the mystery of the esoteric Buddhism and Tâoism.

In par. 4 'The guarding what is soft' is derived from the use of 'the soft lips' in hiding and preserving the hard and strong teeth.

Par. 5 gives the gist of the chapter:–Man's always keeping before him the ideal of the Tâo, and, without purpose, simply doing whatever he finds to do; Tâo-like and powerful in all his sphere of action.

I have followed the reading of the last character but one, which is given by Ziâo Hung instead of that found in Ho-shang Kung and Wang Pî.

53

53. 1. If I were suddenly to become known, and (put into a position to) conduct (a government) according to the Great Tâo, what I should be most afraid of would be a boastful display.

2. The great Tâo (or way) is very level and easy; but people love the by-ways.

3. Their court(-yards and buildings) shall be well kept, but their fields shall be ill-cultivated, and their granaries very empty. They shall wear elegant and ornamented robes, carry a sharp sword at their girdle, pamper themselves in eating and drinking, and have a superabundance of property and wealth;–such (princes) may be called robbers and boasters. This is contrary to the Tâo surely!

益證, 'Increase of Evidence.' The chapter contrasts government by the Tâo with that conducted in a spirit of ostentation and by oppression.

In the 'I' of par. 1 does Lâo-dze speak of himself? I think he does. Wû Khäng understands it of 'any man,' i.e. anyone in the exercise of government;–which is possible. What is peculiar to my version is the pregnant meaning given to 有知, common enough in the mouth of Confucius. I have adopted it here because of a passage in Liû Hsiang's Shwo-wän (XX, 13 b), where Lâo-dze is made to say 'Excessive is the difficulty of practising the Tâo at the present time,' adding that the princes of his age would not receive it from him. On the 'Great Tâo,' see chapters 25, 34, et al. From the twentieth book of Han Fei (12 b and 13 a) I conclude that he had the whole of this chapter in his copy of our King, but he broke it up, after his fashion, into fragmentary utterances, confused and confounding. He gives also some remarkable various readings, one of which (竽, instead of Ho-shang Kung and Wang Pî's

夸, character 48) is now generally adopted. The passage is quoted in the Khang-hsî dictionary under 竽 with this reading.

54

54. 1. What (Tâo's) skilful planter plants Can never be uptorn; What his skilful arms enfold, From him can ne'er be borne. Sons shall bring in lengthening line, Sacrifices to his shrine.

2. Tâo when nursed within one's self, His vigour will make true;

And where the family it rules What riches will accrue! The neighbourhood where it prevails In thriving will abound; And when 'tis seen throughout the state, Good fortune will be found. Employ it the kingdom o'er, And men thrive all around.

3. In this way the effect will be seen in the person, by the observation of different cases; in the family; in the neighbourhood; in the state; and in the kingdom.

4. How do I know that this effect is sure to hold thus all under the sky? By this (method of observation).

修觀, 'The Cultivation (of the Tâo), and the Observation (of its Effects).' The sentiment of the first paragraph is found in the 27th and other previous chapters,–that the noiseless and imperceptible acting of the Tâo is irresistible in its influence; and this runs through to the end of the chapter with the additional appeal to the influence of its effects. The introduction of the subject of sacrifices, a religious rite, though not presented to the Highest Object, will strike the reader as peculiar in our King.

The Teh mentioned five times in par. 2 is the 'virtue' of the Tâo embodied in the individual, and extending from him in all the spheres of his occupation, and is explained differently by Han Fei according to its application; and his example I have to some extent followed.

The force of pars. 3 and 4 is well given by Ho-shang Kung. On the first clause he says, 'Take the person of one who cultivates the Tâo, and compare it with that of one who does not cultivate it;–which is in a state of decay? and which is in a state of preservation?'

55

55. 1. He who has in himself abundantly the attributes (of the Tâo) is like an infant. Poisonous insects will not sting him; fierce beasts will not seize him; birds of prey will not strike him.

2. (The infant's) bones are weak and its sinews soft, but yet its grasp is firm. It knows not yet the union of male and female, and yet its virile member may be excited;–showing the perfection of its physical essence. All day long it will cry without its throat becoming hoarse;–showing the harmony (in its constitution).

3. To him by whom this harmony is known, (The secret of) the unchanging (Tâo) is shown, And in the knowledge wisdom finds its throne. All life-increasing arts to evil turn; Where the mind makes the vital breath to burn, (False) is the strength, (and o'er it we should mourn.)

4. When things have become strong, they (then) become old, which may be said to be contrary to the Tâo. Whatever is contrary to the Tâo soon ends.

玄符, 'The Mysterious Charm;' meaning, apparently, the entire passivity of the Tâo.

With pars. 1 and 2, compare what is said about the infant in chapters 10 and 20, and about the immunity from dangers such as here described of the disciple of the Tâo in Ch. 50. My 'evil' in the second triplet of par. 3 has been translated by 'felicity;' but a reference to the Khang-hsî dictionary will show that the meaning which I give to 祥 is well authorised. It is the only meaning allowable here. The third and fourth 曰 in this paragraph appear in Ho-shang Kung's text as 日, and he comments on the clauses accordingly;

but 曰 is now the received reading. Some light is thrown on this paragraph and the next by an apocryphal conversation attributed to Lâo-dze in Liû Hsiang's Shwo-wän, X, 4 a.

56

56. 1. He who knows (the Tâo) does not (care to) speak (about it); he who is (ever ready to) speak about it does not know it.

2. He (who knows it) will keep his mouth shut and close the portals (of his nostrils). He will blunt his sharp points and unravel the complications of things; he will attemper his brightness, and bring himself into agreement with the obscurity (of others). This is called 'the Mysterious Agreement.'

3. (Such an one) cannot be treated familiarly or distantly; he is beyond all consideration of profit or injury; of nobility or meanness:–he is the noblest man under heaven.

玄德, 'The Mysterious Excellence.' The chapter gives us a picture of the man of Tâo, humble and retiring, oblivious of himself and of other men, the noblest man under heaven.

Par. 1 is found in Kwang-dze (XIII, 20 b), not expressly mentioned, as taken from Lâo-dze, but at the end of a string of sentiments, ascribed to 'the Master,' some of them, like the two clauses here, no doubt belonging to him, and the others, probably Kwang-dze's own.

Par. 2 is all found in chapters 4 and 52, excepting the short clause in the conclusion.

57

57. 1. A state may be ruled by (measures of) correction; weapons of war maybe used with crafty dexterity; (but) the kingdom is made one's own (only) by freedom from action and purpose.

2. How do I know that it is so? By these facts:–In the kingdom the multiplication of prohibitive enactments increases the poverty of the people; the more implements to add to their profit that the people have, the greater disorder is there in the state and clan; the more acts of crafty dexterity that men possess, the more do strange contrivances appear; the more display there is of legislation, the more thieves and robbers there are.

3. Therefore a sage has said, 'I will do nothing (of purpose), and the people will be transformed of themselves; I will be fond of keeping still, and the people will of themselves become correct. I will take no trouble about it, and the people will of themselves become rich; I will manifest no ambition, and the people will of themselves attain to the primitive simplicity.'

淳風, 'The Genuine Influence.' The chapter shows how government by the Tâo is alone effective, and of universal application; contrasting it with the failure of other methods.

After the 'weapons of war' in par. 1, one is tempted to take 'the sharp implements' in par. 2 as such weapons, but the meaning which I finally adopted, especially after studying chapters 36 and 80, seems more consonant with Lâo-dze's scheme of thought. In the last member of the same paragraph, Ho-shang Kung has the strange reading of 法物,

and uses it in his commentary; but the better text of 法令 is found both in Hwâi-nan and Sze-mâ Khien, and in Wang Pî.

We do not know if the writer were quoting any particular sage in par. 3, or referring generally to the sages of the past;–men like the 'sentence-makers' of Ch. 41.

58

58. 1. The government that seems the most unwise, Oft goodness to the people best supplies;

That which is meddling, touching everything, Will work but ill, and disappointment bring.

Misery!–happiness is to be found by its side! Happiness!–misery lurks beneath it! Who knows what either will come to in the end?

2. Shall we then dispense with correction? The (method of) correction shall by a turn become distortion, and the good in it shall by a turn become evil. The delusion of the people (on this point) has indeed subsisted for a long time.

3. Therefore the sage is (like) a square which cuts no one (with its angles); (like) a corner which injures no one (with its sharpness). He is straightforward, but allows himself no license; he is bright, but does not dazzle.

順 化, 'Transformation according to Circumstances;' but this title does not throw light on the meaning of the chapter; nor are we helped to an understanding of it by Han Fei, with his additions and comments (XI, 3 b, 4 b), nor by Hwâi-nan with his illustrations (XII, 21 a, b). The difficulty of it is increased by its being separated from the preceding chapter of which it is really the sequel. It contrasts still further government by the Tâo, with that by the method of correction. The sage is the same in both chapters, his character and government both marked by the opposites or contraries which distinguish the procedure of the Tâo, as stated in Ch. 40.

59

59. 1. For regulating the human (in our constitution) and rendering the (proper) service to the heavenly, there is nothing like moderation.

2. It is only by this moderation that there is effected an early return (to man's normal state). That early return is what I call the repeated accumulation of the attributes (of the Tâo). With that repeated accumulation of those attributes, there comes the subjugation (of every obstacle to such return). Of this subjugation we know not what shall be the limit; and when one knows not what the limit shall be, he may be the ruler of a state.

3. He who possesses the mother of the state may continue long. His case is like that (of the plant) of which we say that its roots are deep and its flower stalks firm:–this is the way to secure that its enduring life shall long be seen.

守道, 'Guarding the Tâo.' The chapter shows how it is the guarding of the Tâo that ensures a continuance of long life, with vigour and success. The abuse of it and other passages in our King helped on, I must believe, the later Tâoist dreams about the elixir vitae and life-preserving pills. The whole of it, with one or two various readings, is found in Han Fei (VI, 4 b-6 a), who speaks twice in his comments of 'The Book.'

Par. 1 has been translated, 'In governing men and in serving Heaven, there is nothing like moderation.' But by 'Heaven' there is not intended 'the blue sky' above us, nor any personal Power above it, but the Tâo embodied in our constitution, the Heavenly element in our nature. The 'moderation' is the opposite of what we call 'living fast,' 'burning the candle at both ends.'

In par. 2 I must read 復, instead of the more common 服. I find it in Lû Teh-ming, and that it is not a misprint in him appears from his subjoining that it is pronounced like 服. Its meaning is the same as in 復歸其明 in Ch. 52, par. 5. Teh is not 'virtue' in our common meaning of the term, but 'the attributes of the Tâo,' as almost always with Lâo-dze.

In par. 3 'the mother of the state' is the Tâo as in ch. 1, and especially in Ch. 52, par. 1.

60

60. 1. Governing a great state is like cooking small fish.

2. Let the kingdom be governed according to the Tâo, and the manes of the departed will not manifest their spiritual energy. It is not that those manes have not that spiritual energy, but it will not be employed to hurt men. It is not that it could not hurt men, but neither does the ruling sage hurt them.

3. When these two do not injuriously affect each other, their good influences converge in the virtue (of the Tâo).

居 位, 'Occupying the Throne;' occupying it, that is, according to the Tâo, noiselessly and purposelessly, so that the people enjoy their lives, free from all molestation seen and unseen.

Par. 1. That is, in the most quiet and easy manner. The whole of the chapter is given and commented on by Han Fei (VI, 6a-7b); but very unsatisfactorily.

The more one thinks and reads about the rest of the chapter, the more does he agree with the words of Julien:–'It presents the frequent recurrence of the same characters, and appears as insignificant as it is unintelligible, if we give to the Chinese characters their ordinary meaning.'–The reader will observe that we have here the second mention of spirits (the manes; Chalmers, 'the ghosts;' Julien, les démons). See Ch. 39.

Whatever Lâo-dze meant to teach in par. 2, he laid in it a foundation for the superstition of the later and present Tâoism about the spirits of the dead;–such as appeared few years ago in the 'tail-cutting' scare.

61

61. 1. What makes a great state is its being (like) low-lying, down-flowing (stream);–it becomes the centre to which tend (all the small states) under heaven.

2. (To illustrate from) the case of all females:–the female always overcomes the male by her stillness. Stillness may be considered (a sort of) abasement.

3. Thus it is that a great state, by condescending to small states, gains them for itself; and that small states, by abasing themselves to a great state, win it over to them. In the one case the abasement leads to gaining adherents, in the other case to procuring favour.

4. The great state only wishes to unite men together and nourish them; a small state only wishes to be received by, and to serve, the other. Each gets what it desires, but the great state must learn to abase itself

謙德, 'The Attribute of Humility;'–a favourite theme with Lâo-dze; and the illustration of it from the low-lying stream to which smaller streams flow is also a favourite subject with him. The language can hardly but recall the words of a greater than Lâo-dze.–'He that humbleth himself shall be exalted.'

62

62. 1. Tâo has of all things the most honoured place.

No treasures give good men so rich a grace; Bad men it guards, and doth their ill efface.

2. (Its) admirable words can purchase honour; (its) admirable deeds can raise their performer above others. Even men who are not good are not abandoned by it.

3. Therefore when the sovereign occupies his place as the Son of Heaven, and he has appointed his three ducal ministers, though (a prince) were to send in a round symbol-of-rank large enough to fill both the hands, and that as the precursor of the team of horses (in the court-yard), such an offering would not be equal to (a lesson of) this Tâo, which one might present on his knees.

4. Why was it that the ancients prized this Tâo so much? Was it not because it could be got by seeking for it, and the guilty could escape (from the stain of their guilt) by it? This is the reason why all under heaven consider it the most valuable thing.

爲道, 'Practising the Tâo.' 貴道, 'The value set on the Tâo,' would have been a more appropriate title. The chapter sets forth that value in various manifestations of it.

Par. 1. For the meaning of 奧, see Confucian Analects, III, Ch. 13.

Par. 2. I am obliged to adopt the reading of the first sentence of this paragraph given by Hwâi-nan,

美言可以市尊,美行可以加人;–see especially his quotation of it in XVIII, 10 a, as from a superior man, I have not found his reading anywhere else.

Par. 3 is not easily translated, or explained. See the rules on presenting offerings at the court of a ruler or the king, in vol. xxvii of the 'Sacred Books of the East,' p. 84, note 3, and also a narrative in the Zo Kwan under the thirty-third year of duke Hsî.

63

63. 1. (It is the way of the Tâo) to act without (thinking of) acting; to conduct affairs without (feeling the) trouble of them; to taste without discerning any flavour; to consider what is small as great, and a few as many; and to recompense injury with kindness.

2. (The master of it) anticipates things that are difficult while they are easy, and does things that would become great while they are small. All difficult things in the world are sure to arise from a previous state in which they were easy, and all great things from one in which they were small. Therefore the sage, while he never does what is great, is able on that account to accomplish the greatest things.

3. He who lightly promises is sure to keep but little faith; he who is continually thinking things easy is sure to find them difficult. Therefore the sage sees difficulty even in what seems easy, and so never has any difficulties.

思始, 'Thinking in the Beginning.' The former of these two characters is commonly misprinted **恩**, and this has led Chalmers to mistranslate them by 'The Beginning of Grace.' The chapter sets forth the passionless method of the Tâo, and how the sage accordingly accomplishes his objects easily by forestalling in his measures all difficulties. In par. 1 the clauses are indicative, and not imperative, and therefore we have to supplement the text in translating in some such way, as I have done. They give us a cluster of aphorisms illustrating the procedure of the Tâo 'by contraries,' and conclude with one, which is the chief glory of Lâo-dze's teaching, though I must think that its value is somewhat diminished by the method in which he reaches it. It has not the prominence in the later teaching of Tâoist writers which we should expect, nor is it found (so far as I know) in Kwang-dze, Han Fei, or Hwâi-nan. It is quoted, however, twice by Liû Hsiang;–see my note on par. 2 of Ch. 49.

It follows from the whole chapter that the Tâoistic 'doing nothing' was not an absolute quiescence and inaction, but had a method in it.

64

64. 1. That which is at rest is easily kept hold of; before a thing has given indications of its presence, it is easy to take measures against it; that which is brittle is easily broken; that which is very small is easily dispersed. Action should be taken before a thing has made its appearance; order should be secured before disorder has begun.

2. The tree which fills the arms grew from the tiniest sprout; the tower of nine storeys rose from a (small) heap of earth; the journey of a thousand lî commenced with a single step.

3. He who acts (with an ulterior purpose) does harm; he who takes hold of a thing (in the same way) loses his hold. The sage does not act (so), and therefore does no harm; he does not lay hold (so), and therefore does not lose his hold. (But) people in their conduct of affairs are constantly ruining them when they are on the eve of success. If they were careful at the end, as (they should be) at the beginning, they would not so ruin them.

4. Therefore the sage desires what (other men) do not desire, and does not prize things difficult to get; he learns what (other men) do not learn, and turns back to what the multitude of men have passed by. Thus he helps the natural development of all things, and does not dare to act (with an ulterior purpose of his own).

守微, 'Guarding the Minute.' The chapter is a continuation and enlargement of the last. Wû Khäng, indeed, unites the two, blending them together with some ingenious transpositions and omissions, which it is not necessary to discuss. Compare the first part of par. 3 with the last part of par. 1, Ch. 29.

65

65. 1. The ancients who showed their skill in practising the Tâo did so, not to enlighten the people, but rather to make them simple and ignorant.

2. The difficulty in governing the people arises from their having much knowledge. He who (tries to) govern a state by his wisdom is a scourge to it while he who does not (try to) do so is a blessing.

3. He who knows these two things finds in them also his model and rule. Ability to know this model and rule constitutes what we call the mysterious excellence (of a governor). Deep and far-reaching is such mysterious excellence, showing indeed its possessor as opposite to others, but leading them to a great conformity to him.

淳德, 'Pure, unmixed Excellence.' The chapter shows the powerful and beneficent influence of the Tâo in government, in contrast with the applications and contrivances of human wisdom. Compare Ch. 19. My 'simple and ignorant' is taken from Julien. More literally the translation would be 'to make them stupid.' My 'scourge' in par. 2 is also after Julien's 'fléau.'

66

66. 1. That whereby the rivers and seas are able to receive the homage and tribute of all the valley streams, is their skill in being lower than they;–it is thus that they are the kings of them all. So it is that the sage (ruler), wishing to be above men, puts himself by his words below them, and, wishing to be before them, places his person behind them.

2. In this way though he has his place above them, men do not feel his weight, nor though he has his place before them, do they feel it an injury to them.

3. Therefore all in the world delight to exalt him and do not weary of him. Because he does not strive, no one finds it possible to strive with him.

後已, 'Putting one's self Last.' The subject is the power of the Tâo, by its display of humility in attracting men. The subject and the way in which it is illustrated are frequent themes in the King. See chapters 8, 22, 39, 42, 61, et al.

The last sentence of par. 3 is found also in Ch. 22. There seem to be no quotations from the chapter in Han Fei or Hwâi-nan; but Wû Khäng quotes passages from Tung Kung-shû (of the second century B.C.), and Yang Hsiung (B.C. 53-A.D. 18), which seem to show that the phraseology of it was familiar to them. The former says:–'When one places himself in his qualities below others, his person is above them; when he places them behind those of others, his person is before them;' the other, 'Men exalt him who humbles himself below them; and give the precedence to him who puts himself behind them.'

67

67. 1. All the world says that, while my Tâo is great, it yet appears to be inferior (to other systems of teaching). Now it is just its greatness that makes it seem to be inferior. If it were like any other (system), for long would its smallness have been known!

2. But I have three precious things which I prize and hold fast. The first is gentleness; the second is economy; and the third is shrinking from taking precedence of others.

3. With that gentleness I can be bold; with that economy I can be liberal; shrinking from taking precedence of others, I can become a vessel of the highest honour. Now-a-days they give up gentleness and are all for being bold; economy, and are all for being liberal; the hindmost place, and seek only to be foremost;–(of all which the end is) death.

4. Gentleness is sure to be victorious even in battle, and firmly to maintain its ground. Heaven will save its possessor, by his (very) gentleness protecting him.

三寶, 'The Three Precious Things.' This title is taken from par. 2, and suggests to us how the early framer of these titles intended to express by them the subject-matter of their several chapters. The three things are the three distinguishing qualities of the possessor of the Tâo, the three great moral qualities appearing in its followers, the qualities, we may venture to say, of the Tâo itself. The same phrase is now the common designation of Buddhism in China,–the Tri-ratna or Ratnatraya, 'the Precious Buddha,' 'the Precious Law,' and 'the Precious Priesthood (or rather Monkhood) or Church;' appearing also in the

'Tri-sarana,' or 'formula of the Three Refuges,' what Dr. Eitel calls 'the most primitive formula fidei of the early Buddhists, introduced before Southern and Northern Buddhism separated.' I will not introduce the question of whether Buddhism borrowed this designation from Tâoism, after its entrance into China. It is in Buddhism the formula of a peculiar Church or Religion; in Tâoism a rule for the character, or the conduct which the Tâo demands from all men. 'My Tâo' in par. 1 is the reading of Wang Pî; Ho-shang Kung's text is simply a 我. Wang Pî's reading is now generally adopted.

The concluding sentiment of the chapter is equivalent to the saying of Mencius (VII, ii, IV, 2), 'If the ruler of a state love benevolence, he will have no enemy under heaven.' 'Heaven' is equivalent to 'the Tâo, 'the course of events,–Providence, as we should say.

68

68. He who in (Tâo's) wars has skill Assumes no martial port; He who fights with most good will To rage makes no resort. He who vanquishes yet still Keeps from his foes apart; He whose hests men most fulfil Yet humbly plies his art. Thus we say, 'He ne'er contends, And therein is his might.' Thus we say, 'Men's wills he bends, That they with him unite.' Thus we say, 'Like Heaven's his ends, No sage of old more bright.'

配天, 'Matching Heaven.' The chapter describes the work of the practiser of the Tâo as accomplished like that of Heaven, without striving or crying. He appears under the figure of a mailed warrior (士) of the ancient chariot. The chapter is a sequel of the preceding, and is joined on to it by Wû Khäng, as is also the next.

69

69. 1. A master of the art of war has said, 'I do not dare to be the host (to commence the war); I prefer to be the guest (to act on the defensive). I do not dare to advance an inch; I prefer to retire a foot.' This is called marshalling the ranks where there are no ranks; baring the arms (to fight) where there are no arms to bare; grasping the weapon where there is no weapon to grasp; advancing against the enemy where there is no enemy.

2. There is no calamity greater than lightly engaging in war. To do that is near losing (the gentleness) which is so precious. Thus it is that when opposing weapons are (actually) crossed, he who deplores (the situation) conquers.

玄用, 'The Use of the Mysterious (Tâo).' Such seems to be the meaning of the title. The chapter teaches that, if war were carried on, or rather avoided, according to the Tâo, the result would be success. Lâo-dze's own statements appear as so many paradoxes. They are examples of the procedure of the Tâo by 'contraries,' or opposites.

We do not know who the master of the military art referred to was. Perhaps the author only adopted the style of quotation to express his own sentiments.

70

70. 1. My words are very easy to know, and very easy to practise; but there is no one in the world who is able to know and able to practise them.

2. There is an originating and all-comprehending (principle) in my words, and an authoritative law for the things (which I enforce). It is because they do not know these, that men do not know me.

3. They who know me are few, and I am on that account (the more) to be prized. It is thus that the sage wears (a poor garb of) hair cloth, while he carries his (signet of) jade in his bosom.

知難, 'The Difficulty of being (rightly) Known.' The Tâo comprehends and rules all Lâo-dze's teaching, as the members of a clan were all in the loins of their first father (宗), and continue to look up to him; and the people of a state are all under the direction of their ruler; yet the philosopher had to complain of not being known. Lâo-dze's principle and rule or ruler was the Tâo. His utterance here is very important. Compare the words of Confucius in the Analects, XIV, Ch. 37, et al.

Par. 2 is twice quoted by Hwâi-nan, though his text is not quite the same in both cases.

71

71. 1. To know and yet (think) we do not know is the highest (attainment); not to know (and yet think) we do know is a disease.

2. It is simply by being pained at (the thought of) having this disease that we are preserved from it. The sage has not the disease. He knows the pain that would be inseparable from it, and therefore he does not have it.

知病, 'The Disease of Knowing.' Here, again, we have the Tâo working 'by contraries,'–in the matter of knowledge. Compare par. 1 with Confucius's account of what knowledge is in the Analects, 11, Ch. 17. The par. 1 is found in one place in Hwâi-nan, lengthened out by the addition of particles; but the variation is unimportant. In another place, however, he seems to have had the correct text before him.

Par. 2 is in Han Fei also lengthened out, but with an important variation (不病 for 病病), and I cannot construe his text. His 不 is probably a transcriber's error.

72

72. 1. When the people do not fear what they ought to fear, that which is their great dread will come on them.

2. Let them not thoughtlessly indulge themselves in their ordinary life; let them not act as if weary of what that life depends on.

3. It is by avoiding such indulgence that such weariness does not arise.

4. Therefore the sage knows (these things) of himself, but does not parade (his knowledge); loves, but does not (appear to set a) value on, himself. And thus he puts the latter alternative away and makes choice of the former.

愛已, 'Loving one's Self,' This title is taken from the expression in par. 4; and the object of the chapter seems to be to show how such loving should be manifested, and to enforce the lesson by the example of the 'sage,' the true master of the Tâo.

In par. 1 'the great dread' is death, and the things which ought to be feared and may be feared, are the indulgences of the appetites and passions, which, if not eschewed, tend to shorten life and accelerate the approach of death.

Pars. 2 and 3 are supplementary to 1. For 狹, the second character of Ho-shang Kung's text in par. 2, Wang Pî reads 狎, which has the same name as the other; and according to the Khang-hsî dictionary, the two characters are interchangeable. I have also followed Wû Khäng in adopting 狎 for the former of the two 厭 in par. 3. Wû adopted this reading from a commentator Liû of Lü-ling. It gives a good meaning, and is supported by the structure of other sentences made on similar lines. In par. 4 'the sage' must be 'the ruler who is a sage,' a master of the

Tâo, 'the king' of Ch. 25. He 'loves himself,' i.e. his life, and takes the right measures to prolong his life, but without any demonstration that he is doing so.

The above is, I conceive, the correct explanation of the chapter; but as to the Chinese critics and foreign translators of it, it may be said, 'Quot homines, tot sententiae.' In illustration of this I venture to subjoin what is found on it in the old version of the Jesuit missionaries, which has not been previously printed:–

Prima explicatio juxta interpretes.

1. Populus, ubi jam principis iram non timet, nihil non audet ut jugum excutiat, resque communis ad extremum discrimen adducitur.

2. Ambitio principis non faciat terram angustiorem, et vectigalium magnitudine alendo populo insufficientem; numquam populus patriae pertaesus alias terras quaeret.

3. Vitae si non taedet, neque patrii soli taedebit.

4. Quare sanctus sibi semper attentus potentiam suam non ostentat.

5. Quia vere se amat, non se pretiosum facit; vel quia sibi recte consulit non se talem aestimat cujus felicitati et honori infelices populi unice servire debeant, immo potius eum se reputat qui populorum felicitati totum se debeat impendere.

6. Ergo illud resecat, istud amplectitur.

Alia explicatio.

1. Populus si non ita timet principis majestatem, sed facile ad cum accedit, majestas non minuitur, immo ad summum pervenit.

2. Vectigalibus terra si non opprimitur, suâ quisque contentus alias terras non quaeret, si se non vexari populus experitur.

3. Vitae si non taedet, nec patrii soli taedebit.

4. Quare sanctus majestatis fastum non affectat, immo similem se caeteris ostendit.

5. Sibi recte consulens, populorum amans, non se pretiosum et inaccessibilem facit.

6. Quidquid ergo timorem incutere potest, hoc evitat; quod amorem conciliat et benignitatem, se demonstrat hoc eligi et ultro amplectitur.

73

73. 1. He whose boldness appears in his daring (to do wrong, in defiance of the laws) is put to death; he whose boldness appears in his not daring (to do so) lives on. Of these two cases the one appears to be advantageous, and the other to be injurious. But When Heaven's anger smites a man, Who the cause shall truly scan?.

On this account the sage feels a difficulty (as to what to do in the former case).

2. It is the way of Heaven not to strive, and yet it skilfully overcomes; not to speak, and yet it is skilful in (obtaining) a reply; does not call, and yet men come to it of themselves. Its demonstrations are quiet, and yet its plans are skilful and effective. The meshes of the net of Heaven are large; far apart, but letting nothing escape.

任爲, 'Allowing Men to take their Course.' The chapter teaches that rulers should not be hasty to punish, especially by the infliction of death. Though they may seem to err in leniency, yet Heaven does not allow offenders to escape.

While Heaven hates the ill-doer, yet we must not always conclude from Its judgments that every one who suffers from them is an ill-doer; and the two lines which rhyme, and illustrate this point, are equivalent to the sentiment in our Old Book, 'Clouds and darkness are round about Him.' They are ascribed to Lâo-dze by Lieh-dze (VI, 7 a); but, it has been said, that they are quoted by him 'in an entirely different connexion.' But the same text in two different sermons may be said to be in different connexions. In Lieh-dze and our King the lines have the same meaning, and substantially the same application. Indeed Kang

Kan, of our fourth century, the commentator of Lieh-dze, quotes the comment of Wang Pî on this passage, condensing it into, 'Who can know the mind of Heaven? Only the sage can do so.'

74

74. 1. The people do not fear death; to what purpose is it to (try to) frighten them with death? If the people were always in awe of death, and I could always seize those who do wrong, and put them to death, who would dare to do wrong?

2. There is always One who presides over the infliction of death. He who would inflict death in the room of him who so presides over it may be described as hewing wood instead of a great carpenter. Seldom is it that he who undertakes the hewing, instead of the great carpenter, does not cut his own hands!

制惑, 'Restraining Delusion.' The chapter sets forth the inefficiency of capital punishment, and warns rulers against the infliction of it. Who is it that superintends the infliction of death? The answer of Ho-shang Kung is very clear:–'It is Heaven, which, dwelling on high and ruling all beneath, takes note of the transgressions of men.' There is a slight variation in the readings of the second sentence of par. 2 in the texts of Ho-shang Kung and Wang Pî, and the reading adopted by Ziâo Hung differs a little from them both; but the meaning is the same in them all.

This chapter and the next are rightly joined on to the preceding by Wû Khäng.

75

75. 1. The people suffer from famine because of the multitude of taxes consumed by their superiors. It is through this that they suffer famine.

2. The people are difficult to govern because of the (excessive) agency of their superiors (in governing them). It is through this that they are difficult to govern.

3. The people make light of dying because of the greatness of their labours in seeking for the means of living. It is this which makes them think light of dying. Thus it is that to leave the subject of living altogether out of view is better than to set a high value on it.

貪損, 'How Greediness Injures.' The want of the nothing-doing Tâo leads to the multiplication of exactions by the government, and to the misery of the people, so as to make them think lightly of death. The chapter is a warning for both rulers and people.

It is not easy to determine whether rulers, or people, or both, are intended in the concluding sentence of par. 2.

76

76. 1. Man at his birth is supple and weak; at his death, firm and strong. (So it is with) all things. Trees and plants, in their early growth, are soft and brittle; at their death, dry and withered.

2. Thus it is that firmness and strength are the concomitants of death; softness and weakness, the concomitants of life.

3. Hence he who (relies on) the strength of his forces does not conquer; and a tree which is strong will fill the out-stretched arms, (and thereby invites the feller.)

4. Therefore the place of what is firm and strong is below, and that of what is soft and weak is above.

戒强, 'A Warning against (trusting in) Strength.' To trust in one's force is contrary to the Tâo, whose strength is more in weakness and humility.

In par. 1 the two characters which I have rendered by '(so it is with) all things' are found in the texts of both Ho-shang Kung and Wang Pî, but Wû Khäng and Ziâo Hung both reject them. I should also have neglected them, but they are also found in Liû Hsiang's Shwo Wän (X, 4 a), with all the rest of pars. 1 and 2, as from Lâo-dze. They are an anacoluthon, such as is elsewhere found in our King; e.g. 天下之牝 in Ch. 21, par. 2. The 'above' and 'below' in par. 4 seem to be merely a play on the words, as capable of meaning 'more and less honourable.'

77

77. 1. May not the Way (or Tâo) of Heaven be compared to the (method of) bending a bow? The (part of the bow) which was high is brought low, and what was low is raised up. (So Heaven) diminishes where there is superabundance, and supplements where there is deficiency.

2. It is the Way of Heaven to diminish superabundance, and to supplement deficiency. It is not so with the way of man. He takes away from those who have not enough to add to his own superabundance.

3. Who can take his own superabundance and therewith serve all under heaven? Only he who is in possession of the Tâo!

4. Therefore the (ruling) sage acts without claiming the results as his; he achieves his merit and does not rest (arrogantly) in it:–he does not wish to display his superiority.

天道, 'The Way of Heaven;' but the chapter contrasts that way, unselfish and magnanimous, with the way of man, selfish and contracted, and illustrates the point by the method of stringing a bow. This must be seen as it is done in China fully to understand the illustration. I have known great athletes in this country tasked to the utmost of their strength to adjust and bend a large Chinese bow from Peking.

The 'sage' of par. 4 is the 'King' of Ch. 25. Compare what is said of him with Ch. 2, par. 4, et al.

78

78. 1. There is nothing in the world more soft and weak than water, and yet for attacking things that are firm and strong there is nothing that can take precedence of it;–for there is nothing (so effectual) for which it can be changed.

2. Every one in the world knows that the soft overcomes the hard, and the weak the strong, but no one is able to carry it out in practice.

3. Therefore a sage has said, He who accepts his state's reproach, Is hailed therefore its altars' lord; To him who bears men's direful woes They all the name of King accord.'

4. Words that are strictly true seem to be paradoxical.

任信, 'Things to be Believed.' It is difficult to give a short and appropriate translation of this title. The chapter shows how the most unlikely results follow from action according to the Tâo.

Par. 1. Water was Lâo-dze's favourite emblem of the Tâo. Compare chapters 8, 66, et al.

Par. 2. Compare Ch. 36, par. 2.

Par. 3. Of course we do not know who the sage was from whom Lâo-dze got the lines of this paragraph. They may suggest to some readers the lines of Burns, as they have done to me:–

'The honest man, though e'er so poor, Is king o' men for a' that.'

But the Tâoist of Lâo-dze is a higher ideal than Burns's honest man.

Par. 4 is separated from this chapter, and made to begin the next by Wû Khäng.

79

79. 1. When a reconciliation is effected (between two parties) after a great animosity, there is sure to be a grudge remaining (in the mind of the one who was wrong). And how can this be beneficial (to the other)?

2. Therefore (to guard against this), the sage keeps the left-hand portion of the record of the engagement, and does not insist on the (speedy) fulfilment of it by the other party. (So), he who has the attributes (of the Tâo) regards (only) the conditions of the engagement, while he who has not those attributes regards only the conditions favourable to himself.

3. In the Way of Heaven, there is no partiality of love; it is always on the side of the good man.

任契, 'Adherence to Bond or Covenant.' The chapter shows, but by no means clearly, how he who holds fast to the Tâo will be better off in the end than he who will rather try to secure his own interests.

Par. 1 presents us with a case which the statements of the chapter are intended to meet:–two disputants, one good, and the other bad; the latter, though apparently reconciled, still retaining a grudge, and ready to wreak his dissatisfaction, when he has an opportunity. The 爲 = 'for,' 'for the good of.'

Par. 2 is intended to solve the question. The terms of a contract or agreement were inscribed on a slip of wood, which was then divided into two; each party having one half of it. At the settlement, if the halves perfectly fitted to each other, it was carried through. The one who had the right in the dispute has his part of the agreement, but does not insist on it, and is forbearing; the other insists on the conditions being even now altered in his favour. The characters by which this last case is expressed, are very enigmatical, having reference to the satisfaction of the government dues of Lâo-dze's time,–a subject into which it would take much space to go.

Par. 3 decides the question by the action of Heaven, which is only another name for the course of the Tâo.

80

80. 1. In a little state with a small population, I would so order it, that, though there were individuals with the abilities of ten or a hundred men, there should be no employment of them; I would make the people, while looking on death as a grievous thing, yet not remove elsewhere (to avoid it).

2. Though they had boats and carriages, they should have no occasion to ride in them; though they had buff coats and sharp weapons, they should have no occasion to don or use them.

3. I would make the people return to the use of knotted cords (instead of the written characters).

4. They should think their (coarse) food sweet; their (plain) clothes beautiful; their (poor) dwellings places of rest; and their common (simple) ways sources of enjoyment.

5. There should be a neighbouring state within sight, and the voices of the fowls and dogs should be heard all the way from it to us, but I would make the people to old age, even to death, not have any intercourse with it.

獨立, 'Standing Alone.' The chapter sets forth what Lâo-dze conceived the ancient government of simplicity was, and what he would have government in all time to be. He does not use the personal pronoun 'I' as the subject of the thrice-recurring 使, but it is most natural to suppose that he is himself that subject; and he modestly supposes himself in charge of a little state and a small population. The reader can judge for himself of the consummation that would be arrived at;–a people rude and uninstructed, using quippos, abstaining from war and all travelling, kept aloof from intercourse even with their neighbours, and without the appliances of what we call civilisation.

The text is nearly all found in Sze-mâ Khien and Kwang-dze. The first member of par. 1, however, is very puzzling. The old Jesuit translators, Julien, Chalmers, and V. von Strauss, all differ in their views of it. Wû Khäng and Ziâo Hung take what I have now rendered by 'abilities,' as meaning 'implements of agriculture,' but their view is based on a custom of the Han dynasty, which is not remote enough for the purpose, and on the suppression, after Wang Pî, of a 人 in Ho-shang Kung's text.

81

81. 1. Sincere words are not fine; fine words are not sincere. Those who are skilled (in the Tâo) do not dispute (about it); the disputatious are not skilled in it. Those who know (the Tâo) are not extensively learned; the extensively learned do not know it.

2. The sage does not accumulate (for himself). The more that he expends for others, the more does he possess of his own; the more that he gives to others, the more does he have himself.

3. With all the sharpness of the Way of Heaven, it injures not; with all the doing in the way of the sage he does not strive.

顯質, 'The Manifestation of Simplicity.' The chapter shows how quietly and effectively the Tâo proceeds, and by contraries in a way that only the master of it can understand. The author, says Wû Khäng, 'sums up in this the subject-matter of the two Parts of his Treatise, showing that in all its five thousand characters, there is nothing beyond what is here said.'

Par. 2 suggests to Dr. Chalmers the well-known lines of Bunyan as an analogue of it:–

'A man there was, though some did count him mad, The more he gave away, the more he had.'

Wû Khäng brings together two sentences from Kwang-dze (XXXIII, 21 b, 22 a), written evidently with the characters of this text in mind, which, as from a Tâoist mint, are a still better analogue, and I venture to put them into rhyme:–

'Amassing but to him a sense of need betrays; He hoards not, and thereby his affluence displays.'

I have paused long over the first pair of contraries in par. 3 (利 and 害). Those two characters primarily mean 'sharpness' and 'wounding by cutting;' they are also often used in the sense of I being beneficial,' and 'being injurious;'–'contraries,' both of them. Which 'contrary' had Lâo-dze in mind? I must think the former, though differing in this from all previous translators. The Jesuit version is, 'Celestis Tâo natura ditat omnes, nemini nocet;' Julien's, 'Il est utile aux êtres, et ne leur nuit point;' Chalmers's, 'Benefits and does not injure;' and V. von Strauss's, 'Des Himmels Weise ist wolthun und nicht beschddigen.'